D0206468

BY TIM WYNNE-JONES

LORD OF THE FRIES

Lord of the Fries

AND OTHER STORIES BY
TIM WYNNE-JONES

A GROUNDWOOD BOOK
DOUGLAS & McINTYRE   TORONTO VANCOUVER

Groundwood Books/Douglas & McIntyre Ltd.
585 Bloor Street West, Toronto, Ontario M6G 1K5

We acknowledge the financial support of the Canada Council
for the Arts, the Ontario Arts Council and the Government of
Canada through the Book Publishing Industry Development
Program for our publishing activities.

Canadian Cataloguing in Publication Data

Wynne-Jones, Tim
Lord of the fries and other stories

A Groundwood book.
ISBN 0-88899-274-2

I. Title.

PS8595.Y59L67 1999   jC813'.54   C98-932372-2
PZ7.W96Lo 1999

Chapter illustrations by Tim Wynne-Jones
Cover illustration by Marion Stuck
Design by Michael Solomon
Printed and bound in Canada
by Webcom Ltd.

ACKNOWLEDGEMENTS

"Lord of the Fries," in a shorter, quite different version, was first read as part of the 1995 Helen E. Stubbs Memorial Lecture entitled onceuponatime@here.now, presented at the Osborne Collection of the Lillian H. Smith Children's Library in Toronto. I would like to thank Margaret Crawford Maloney for inviting me there. I'd like to thank Geoff and Carolee Mason, who were kind enough to read an earlier version of "Ick" and impart some advice. The same goes to Mary Rubio, who read a draft of "The Anne Rehearsals." I'm indebted to Jane Kaszczynec and Norca. When Jane told me how they met, I knew I had to use it in a story some day, and I did at the end of "The Pinhole Camera." Lewis Wynne-Jones offered some good advice on that story as well. Thanks, Lewis. Finally, I'd also like to say *merci bien* to Pauline Morency, who supplied me with the French for "The Chinese Babies," and to Wendy Wynne-Jones and Paul W. Birt, who supplied me with the snippets of Welsh in the same story.

This book is for
Michael and Coral Nault
for all their many kindnesses

CONTENTS

LORD OF THE FRIES

You could tell right away, even without looking at the license plate, that they weren't from around here. The kid was around eight or nine, wearing shorts the colour of eggplant. He had matching Nikes. His folks opened up a road map as soon as they pulled into the parking lot at Barb and Bruno's Burger Barn. They gave the kid money for fries.

I was sitting at a picnic table fending off wasps and waiting for Carrie. I already had my fries, so I knew what that poor little purple kid didn't.

The Lord of the Fries was in one of his moods.

"Yeah?"

"Fries, please."

"Oh, that's special! Fries. Great. Ya want 'em in a crate? Ya want 'em by the yard?"

"Excuse me, sir?"

"How many fries, Sunshine? Twenty-four? A pocketful? Help me out here."

"L-L-Large, please."

But by now the kid wasn't sure he wanted any fries at all. By now that kid was wishing he'd never been born.

Carrie arrived for the finale, when the kid's folks yelled at the Lord of the Fries and said they'd take their business elsewhere.

"Come along, Nigel," said the father, leading the boy back to the car. The father, in khakis and Ray Bans, looked like the Man from Gap. The mother was more like the United Colors of Benetton, from her lime-green mules all the way up to her frizzy scarlet hair. Her face was scarlet, too. She wasn't finished with the Lord of the Fries.

"What is your name?" she demanded, rummaging around in her giant sunflower-yellow handbag for a pen and paper. "I've a good mind to report you to the Chamber of Commerce."

Whatever the Lord of the Fries said to her, it wasn't his name.

"You repulsive little man!" she exclaimed, clamping her handbag shut. She headed off towards the car, but she couldn't resist unloading some of her venom as she stomped past Carrie and me.

"Who does he think he is?" she said.

I should have just shrugged it off, but I felt I had to say something. "It's nothing personal, ma'am. He's like that to everyone."

"He's the Lord of the Fries," said Carrie.

The woman stopped in her tracks. She hurled a glance back towards the Burger Barn, but Fries had retreated into his hole. "Miserable little mealworm," she muttered.

I couldn't help myself. I had to defend him. He may be nasty, but he's ours.

"You wouldn't say that, ma'am, if you knew what he's been through."

A green light seemed to come on in her eyes. "Something bad?"

I nodded, looking away sadly.

She perched on the edge of the picnic table. "Some kind of industrial accident?"

She was referring to his face. On one side it looked as if maybe he'd treated himself to a hot-grease facial.

"Well, not that so much as what happened after," I said. I SOSed Carrie for help. She was on the verge of splitting a gut.

"Hmm." The woman had a scheming kind of look on her face. "Something so terrible he has to be rude to complete strangers?" But she didn't sound angry anymore; she sounded downright intrigued. I didn't know what to say. Carrie came to my rescue.

"It's a terrible story," she said.

"Heart-wrenching," I added.

The woman's painted-on eyebrow arched a bit higher. She looked back towards the Burger Barn, up at the peeling sign with Bruno's awful painting of a smiling hamburger on it. She looked beyond the parking lot at the maple trees filled with offshore breeze, the church steeple down on Lakeside. She squinted at the wedge of Big Rideau Lake you could see between the old tin roofs of Main Street. When she returned her attention to us, she was beaming as if she'd just decided to buy the whole town.

"Such a pretty village," she said. "And yet Tragedy can strike anywhere, can't it?"

I nodded, a little uneasily. I wasn't sure where she was going with this.

She was clutching her handbag, looking thought-ful. "This Lord of the Fries," she said. "Would you say his story is a Real Tearjerker?"

"Oh, yeah," said Carrie. She turned to me.

"Totally unbelievable," I said.

The Man from Gap honked his horn. But the woman was digging in her handbag again. "I love a good Human-Interest story," she said. The way she said "human interest" made it sound as if she were talking about rodent entrails.

She wore a lot of gold bracelets that jangled as she laid a business card down on the table between us. We stared at it.

Greer Hunter, Editor
People Like Us Magazine

Stunned, we looked up at her. The tanned skin around her sparkly eyes crinkled with pleasure. "I'm just dying to hear this story," she said.

Luckily the Man from Gap blew the horn again. Greer Hunter's lips tightened. "But obviously there's not time right now."

Our relief was short-lived.

"I'll meet with you," she said. "Right here. Tomorrow around noon?" It was an order.

As far as I was concerned, it was time to bail out. I started to explain. "We were just —"

But Carrie cut me off. "— going up to my cottage."

The Hunter lady looked truly disappointed. And the whole thing might have ended right there if Carrie had only kept her big mouth shut.

"Unfortunately our cottage is really far away, up at Wild Lake."

Greer Hunter's eyes lit up. "Why, that's where

we're heading!" she said. Next thing we knew, she was digging the map out of her purse. She spread it out on the table, knocked over my fries. She didn't even notice.

"Where, precisely?" she demanded.

Carrie glanced my way. I was glaring at her. She gulped and pointed to tiny little Solitude Bay.

"Actually, we're not going for three days," I said hastily.

"Perfect," said Greer. "We've taken the place on Dortchen Point for the week." A peach-coloured fingernail located the spot. "Here it is. Directly across the lake."

"The big A-frame?" Carrie asked.

"So you know the place? Good. You won't have any trouble finding me."

Behind her the power window of the car rolled down. "For God's sake, Greer," said the man.

"I'm coming, Roger," she said sweetly enough, though you could tell she wasn't a woman who liked being told what to do.

Her scowl vanished when she looked at us. "I'm counting on you girls," she said. "You absolutely *must* tell me the Tragic Tale of the Lord of the Fries."

Then she turned on her mules and sashayed back towards the car. She stopped and looked our way again.

"Oh, did I say? There's very good money in it for you."

They roared away, throwing up a cloud of dust that left Carrie and me coughing. When the dust settled, Carrie was smiling at me with dollar signs in her eyes.

"But, Carrie," I said, "we don't even know his name!"

"I bet it's something like Leroy."

I made a face.

"How about Norbert? Abdul? Gladys?"

It's hard to stay mad at Carrie, but I did my best.

"Thanks to you, she knows where your cottage is," I said. "If we don't show up, she'll swoop down on us."

Carrie threw up her hands in disgust. "Who started it?" she said. "You with your sob story, that's who. But what I'm saying, Sam, is who cares who started it. Do you know what the circulation of *People Like Us* is? About twenty gazillion. We'll be famous! Famous and *rich*."

I busied myself picking up the fries the Hunter lady had spilled on the table. Famous and rich sounded okay. And I liked the idea of writing a story. I love making up stories.

I held a perfect golden fry up to the sun. We do not wreck his lordship's handiwork with ketchup. Is that why I came to his defense? I mean, after all, he is a genius.

Carrie snatched the fry from my hand. "And the Lord of the Fries'll be famous, too," she said.

I looked uncertainly towards the Burger Barn.

"Didn't you hear what she said, Sam?" Carrie's eyes were wild. "Good money. Thousands of dollars, I bet."

Carrie gobbled up my fry. I chose another, a long one, suitable for making a point.

"Point one," I said, poking her in the chest with the fry. "She said good money for a *good* story. A tearjerker. A *real* tearjerker. For all we know, Fries acts like he does because he's got a stomach ulcer or something. You think *People Like Us Magazine* cares about some short-order cook's bowel problems?"

I didn't have a point two. I ate my pointer. It was cold.

Carrie looked grimly determined, just like she did when we ran in the track meet that spring. It was that I-can-win-it-all-as-long-as-nobody-gets-in-my-way-and-God-help-them-if-they-do expression.

She crossed her arms, stuck out her bottom lip. "Couldn't we at least try?"

The phone inside the Burger Barn rang. We listened, expecting to hear Fries sounding off. All we heard was a murmur. Very unusual. The Lord of the Fries snarls, rants, fumes, seethes and yells. He does not murmur. We were on our feet in a flash and sneaking towards the food window, where we crouched out of sight, listening.

"You tell him to see me," said Fries. "If he so much as...okay, I'm sorry..."

Sorry? The Lord of the Fries *sorry!*

There was a long sigh. "Yeah, yeah, yeah. You just hang tight. Hear what I'm sayin'? I'll get there as soon as I can..."

Then his voice got low and we didn't catch the rest before — click — he hung up.

Only then did it occur to us that our present situation was not, strategically, a good one. We looked up into his lordship's beady eyes. He was leaning out over the counter, glaring at us.

"You drop somethin'?" he asked.

Sheepishly we stood up. Carrie and I played a little eye Ping-Pong. I lost, took a deep breath.

"Hey, Fries," I said. "That woman sure was rude, huh?" He glared at me, waiting. So much for small talk. I decided on Plan B, the direct approach.

"How would you like to be famous?" I asked.

His face clouded over. He started to growl.

"Okay," I said, "you've made your point. But, well, my friend and I have been coming here for three years, and we suddenly realized we don't even know your name."

He shook his head and turned to the cutting board on the back counter, where he had a huge pile of potatoes washed and ready.

"Is it Leroy?" said Carrie. No response. "How about Norbert?" He just kept slicing, his hand a blur, his knife flashing.

"Abdul? Gladys? Igor?"

His knife smacked down hard on the cutting board. He glanced back scornfully. "Mind your own beeswax," he grouched.

I backed off. But not Carrie. "So is Beeswax the last name?"

"Yeah," he said, turning back to his work. "It's the last name you're gonna get outa me!"

We retreated to our picnic table.

"Look," I said, "when we get up to the cottage, we just go over to Dortchen Point and tell the Hunter lady we were pulling her leg."

Carrie raised an eyebrow. "You want to tell her that?" She had a point. I didn't imagine Greer Hunter liked having her leg pulled. "Don't give up so easy," she said. "How hard can it be to find out about somebody in a town this size?"

Just then Barb and Bruno drove up in their old blue van and began unloading supplies. Fries came out the back door with his baseball cap low over his eyes. We'd seen him heft gigantic bags of potatoes over his knobbly shoulder. He may be small, but he's mighty strong.

This time, to our surprise, he merely tipped his cap towards his bosses and headed across the parking lot.

"Trouble?" said Bruno.

"Yeah, yeah, yeah," said Fries. He was walking with his chin out and his wiry arms pumping, like a man with a mission. He was wearing cowboy boots, which kicked up puffs of dust as he walked. His jeans were tight, his legs as skinny as rope, his white T-shirt was blotched with sweat. He looked about as tough as a guy four foot nothing could possibly look.

"You show 'em, Fries," said Barb.

"Come on," said Carrie, her eyes wide. I grabbed my fries, and we were off in pursuit.

So there we were tracking the Lord of the Fries to Trouble — wherever that was. We really had to motor to keep up.

"He walks funny," I said. "Like a newt."

"Maybe he is a newt," said Carrie. "Maybe he lives in a log."

"And maybe a snake bit off his tail," I said, "and it never grew back because of the spell."

"What spell?"

"The one that turned him into a newt. But it only half worked, so he's part newt and part human."

"And that's why he's so mad!" said Carrie. I nodded.

We passed a trash can, and Carrie lobbed my empty fries container at it but missed by a mile. I stopped to pick it up, and then we really had to race to keep up. We started to giggle. Fries didn't notice us. Clearly he had other things on his mind.

I was feeling better. Now that we were actually doing something, it was kind of fun. Just a game, after all. And it was summer. What else did we have to do?

"Who knows?" I said, huffing a bit. "My mother says everyone has a story inside them somewhere."

"Now you're talking, girl," said Carrie. "Who's to say Fries' story isn't *People Like Us* material?"

I wish she hadn't mentioned the magazine. Right away I saw the Hunter lady's face in my mind's eye. That smile that looked like she was going to eat you for supper, the peach-coloured claws perfect for picking through a person's carcass for human interest. But then I saw those same claws handing me an oversized cheque. Enough to buy a laptop computer! Then I would be a real writer.

The Lord of the Fries headed uptown to the highway, where he turned east towards the stretch where the big-name fast-food places were all lined up in a row.

"Maybe he's gonna take on McDonald's single-handed."

"Yeah," said Carrie. "French fries at thirty paces!"

But his destination was the Dairy Queen. And

before we even got there, we heard loud voices coming from inside. Next thing we knew, some guy was backing through the door. The Lord of the Fries was in his face, jumping up and down like an irritated wallaby, poking the big guy in the chest and calling him every name under the sun. The guy was a real Quarter Pounder with all the trimmings. A Quarter Pounder in a bad suit. Skinny little Fries only came up to the guy's chest, but he came up to it again and again. We watched in disbelief as he drove him right out into the parking lot. A lot of other people were watching, too, leaning against their cars, licking ice creams and slurping shakes.

The amazing thing is that Quarter Pounder was totally intimidated. He made a lot of noise as if he were tough, but the Lord of the Fries had him on the run. He laughed at the guy. Well, cackled. Then the guy suddenly noticed other people were watching, and his face turned beet red. He straightened his tie — ow! what a tie — and with one last curse he stomped off towards his car. A chocolate Cadillac.

"And good riddance!" Fries yelled after him. Then he looked around at the gawkers. His gaze landed on us and narrowed to a laser beam. "If you clowns are lookin' for your clones, they're down at B and B's making a nuisance of themselves."

Everybody around us got right back to licking and slurping and minding their own business.

Meanwhile, Quarter Pounder squealed out of the Dairy Queen onto the highway. There was writing on the side of the chocolate Cadillac.

JACK PRINCE MOTORS
for one prince of a deal

Fries stepped back into the Dairy Queen. Carrie and I raced for the door only to find him blocking it, his arms crossed on his chest, his pointy cowboy boot tapping impatiently. We smiled and waved and made as if we were leaving, but we darted back pretty darn quick. Unfortunately, not quick enough. When we looked inside, he was gone. There was nobody there. Nobody even at the counter.

◆

"What do we know so far?" I said. Carrie flipped open her notebook. We were at the Burger Barn again, at our favourite table, the one farthest from the garbage can. Carrie had spent the day before in the city with her mom and baby brother, but she had some news anyway.

"Jack Prince used to be on the city council. But he got into some hot water a few years back, which lost him his seat in the last election."

"What kind of hot water?"

Carrie shrugged. "Mom couldn't remember exactly. A messy divorce or something."

"Scandal. Perfect! So how does the Lord of the Fries fit in?"

Carrie was thinking hard. "Maybe it wasn't a messy divorce. Maybe...maybe it was a hot car ring."

"That's more like it," I said. My mind went into overdrive. "Maybe Jack Prince was using his dealership as a front for selling stolen cars. And Fries was in on it!"

"Which is where he got his face fried," said Carrie, "spinning out of control in a high-speed chase."

"And now," I said, jumping in, "now Prince is trying to cut Fries out of the operation."

"Yes!" said Carrie, beaming with satisfaction.

We have a kind of tag team imagination, Carrie and I. It's fun, but right now what we needed was some cold, hard facts.

I glanced at the Burger Barn window. Fries was filling up a mustard container. Not exactly what you'd call heart-wrenching material. I shook my head sadly.

"We can't give up," said Carrie. "What did you find?"

I opened my notebook. "Well, here's something. Toad wondered if maybe Fries met Bruno in the circus."

"Bruno was in the circus?"

"That's what Toad said. He was a strongman."

"What d'ya think Fries did?" said Carrie, her eyes lighting up. "Maybe he was a flame swallower, and one day he missed and lit his face on fire!"

I laughed. Then Greer Hunter's face floated into my mind. "Oh, Carrie," I said, "we have got to find out what really happened."

We looked towards the Barn. Fries was filling the ketchup container. I shuddered. "The congealed blood of last night's unwary victims," I said in my ghastliest voice.

He stopped and glared, as if maybe he had heard me. We waved. He shook his head and went back to work.

"What happened with the car idea?" said Carrie.

I shook my head, scowling at the memory. "Disastrous!" I said.

The idea had seemed pretty crafty when we'd cooked it up the night before last. The Lord of the Fries always parked his car out behind the Burger Barn. His vehicle was hardly fit for royalty. It looked more like a rusting tank. It was stripped of chrome, no hubcaps, coat hanger for an antenna. One of the windows was covered with cardboard and tape. There were blotches of primer paint where he had fixed up the body, but you could tell the rust was going to win in the end.

The day before, I had written down the license plate number and waited for Constable Giroux to come down from the cop shop for his usual lunch. I showed him the license number.

"I've got to find the owner of this car," I told him.

He looked concerned. "Why's that, Sam?"

"He splashed me when it was raining the other day," I said. "I had on my best party stuff. He has to pay for the dry cleaning, right?"

Constable Giroux wiped the burger juice off his fingers and took the notebook. He sucked on his teeth while he stared at the license number. Then he looked up at the rusty heap at the back of the lot and grinned.

"You're in luck," he said. "There's the vehicle now."

I pretended to be surprised.

"You want me to arrest Fries?" he said.

I looked towards the Barn. Fries was leaning on

the counter, watching us. I looked back at the cop, shook my head and leaned in close. "Okay, so he didn't splash me. I'm just trying to find out something about him."

"Like what?"

"Like his name, for starters. And how he got to be so mad."

Constable Giroux made a hard sniffing noise as if maybe a bit of onion had gone up his nose. He wiped it, took a peek in his napkin to see what he'd discharged, then folded up the napkin real tight. If this display was meant to get rid of me, it almost worked. But I managed to keep my breakfast down and wait him out. Constable Giroux looked me straight in the eye.

"I promised not to blow his cover," he whispered. "But if you swear that it won't go any farther than this table, I'll let you in on a little secret."

Carrie gulped as I repeated the constable's remark. "Then what'd he say?"

"He said that Fries was an undercover cop from New York. Ratted on a big-time mafioso and he's hiding out here till things cool down."

Carrie's jaw dropped with a satisfying clunk. Then she noticed my frown, and her nose curled up. "It's not true?"

I shook my head. "He sucked me right in. And as if that wasn't bad enough, Giroux turned to Fries and said, 'Ain't that right, Fries? You're an undercover cop from the Big Apple?'

"And Fries yells, 'I'm the worm in the Big Apple.'"

Carrie's shoulders slumped. "I bet they had a good laugh over that."

"Oh, Giroux laughed. But Fries didn't. He just gave me that look like he was going to slice, dice and deep-fry me. I felt like a complete goof."

Carrie harrumphed, but you could see she was thinking. "This is actually good," she said. I failed to see why. "Because it indicates that there must be some big secret."

I wasn't so sure. "I asked Bruno and Barb first thing this morning, before Fries arrived. They wouldn't tell me his name. I asked them why he's so mad all the time, and Bruno said, 'Ah, that's just the way his jib is cut.'"

Carrie's face flew into this major pain warp. "What's his jib?" she asked squeamishly.

"That's what I asked. Bruno laughed his head off. It's an expression, I guess. Means that's just the kind of guy he is — something like that."

Carrie looked down in the dumps. I knew how she felt. We were getting nowhere fast and becoming the laughing stock of town in the bargain. It wasn't fair. Tomorrow morning we were heading up to Solitude Bay, a trip that we had been looking forward to for a month. Except now it loomed before us like a math test.

"We've got to get something on him for the Hunter lady," said Carrie.

A loud beeping noise caught our attention. A pop truck was backing into the Burger Barn lot. The guy got out and delivered a few cases of pop to the back door. Fries was there to receive them. Big deal. I lost interest until Carrie almost wrenched my arm off.

The pop guy was making Fries sign for the shipment.

Voom!

We intercepted the pop guy just as he was climbing into his truck. By then Fries was back in the Barn.

"Can we see that?" I asked.

The guy was folding up the invoice. "This? Why?"

"We've never seen one before," said Carrie, as if it were an exotic plant or something. The guy rolled his eyes, but he let us take a look.

Voom!

Our eyes located the signature like heat-seeking missiles.

There it was: a squiggle. A long, bumpy squiggle without a single recognizable letter.

"This might be an *i*," said Carrie.

But the pop guy snatched back the invoice before we got any further. "You girls should think about getting out of the sun," he said.

We plopped down at our table as he drove off. I brought my fist down so hard I made my can of Canada Dry jump.

Some kid was just leaving the food window with a pile of stuff. He asked for extra straws.

"Yeah, yeah, yeah," said Fries, thrusting a mittful of straws at him. "You got enough straws there to suck your brains out."

The kid just yeah-yeah-yeahed him back. A regular, like us.

"What about his tattoo?" said Carrie. "Maybe it'll give us a hint."

Good thinking. "Like maybe it'll say he was in the Marines or something?"

"Right. And was caught in vicious crossfire in the Santa Banana Islands!"

Well, who knew? It was worth a try. Fries had this big tattoo on his right arm. We had never really taken a close look. Until now we'd never paid Fries' personal life much attention.

From the look on his face when we arrived at the window, he didn't seem to like how much attention we were giving him.

"Could I have a glass of water?" said Carrie. Brilliant. You *never* asked for water. When you asked for water, what you got was a lecture, and a lecture might give us time for a good long gander at his arm.

As it turned out, we didn't need much time.

"What is that? A newt?" I asked.

He looked down at the floor before he realized where I was pointing.

"It's a dragon!" he said. He poked at the skin on his upper arm, at the picture embroidered there. "See the fire and smoke?" he said.

The fire and smoke made it look as if the newt was blowing bubble gum. It was a pretty bad tattoo.

"It looks like it's blowing bubbles," I said.

I thought he was going to blow up himself then. The muscles on his neck stood out, his crew cut seemed to stand on end, and smoke came out his ears — I swear! Then something happened. He closed his eyelids tight and grabbed the edge of the counter and held on till his fingers turned blue. Then he let out this long, slow, whistling breath. When it was over, he looked almost calm.

"You two're full of questions, ain't ya?" he said, his thin lips twitching, his eyes shining with mischief. "Followin' me 'round, askin' what my name might be. Don't privacy count for nothin'?"

I looked down, But Carrie wasn't going to be turned away so easily. "Hey, Fries," she said, "you're one of the most colourful guys in town. You're a walking human-interest story. People want to know what makes a guy like you tick. What's wrong with that?"

Fries looked irritated. "Yeah, yeah, yeah," he said. "You think I ain't heard all this before?"

Carrie and I exchanged surprised glances.

"What do you mean, you've heard all this before?" I asked.

Fries looked away, and his face got all pinched and careworn, as if he were remembering something painful. Then he snapped out of it.

"I'll tell you something," he said. "I'm not sure what makes me tick, but I can tell you what makes me sick." He rivetted us in place with his hot little eyes. "It's people who think that other people's business is their business."

It was enough for me. I grabbed Carrie's arm, but she wouldn't budge.

"I'll make a deal with you, Fries," she said. "You tell us your name, and we'll back off. And we'll never tell another living soul."

He stared at Carrie. I stared at Carrie. What was she doing?

Fries scratched his pointy chin. "Not another living soul?" he said.

I guess Carrie must have realized now what she had promised. She didn't answer right away, and when she did, she didn't sound all that convincing.

"No one," she said. I wondered if "no one" was something less than "not another living soul." But Fries seemed to buy it.

"Okay," he said. "It's a deal. I tell ya my name, and then you buzz off. Right?"

Numbly, we nodded.

He looked around to make sure no one was listening or watching. Then he picked up a pen and took a paper napkin and wrote one word on it in big block letters. He swivelled the napkin around so it was facing us. It said:

RUMPELSTILTSKIN

I stared at Carrie, she stared at me. We looked up, but Fries had turned his back on us. He was at his cutting board. He had returned silently to his mountain of potatoes and was cutting like mad, filling up the deep-fryer basket. His knife flashed in the dim light of the cramped kitchen.

"Rumpelstiltskin?" I said.

"Sure," he said. Then he turned. His face was bathed in sweat. He waved a loaded basket at us. "On account of I can turn a roomful of potatoes into gold!"

He started to cackle like a maniac and then plunged the basket into the vat of hot oil. His head soon disappeared in a plume of steam.

♦

Rumpelstiltskin. Why couldn't I shrug it off? I mean, obviously he was kidding.

"Sam, it's a fairy tale."

"I know, I know. But think about it. Those evil little eyes, the way he looks like he's going to tear himself apart any minute..."

Carrie gave up on me. She had to go home anyway and help her mother with baby Gordie. I had to get home myself and pack for the cottage. But I didn't go right away. I went down to the lakefront to do some sitting on a rock and thinking.

What I found myself thinking about was Fries' tattoo. He may have called it a dragon, but it was a newt to me. I'd seen it any number of times before without really noticing it. Maybe that's where I got the idea that he walked like a newt. Who knows? But I couldn't shake the idea of his being not quite human. Just a little squirmy amphibian who had stepped out of the pond and wasn't too sure that dry land was such a hot idea.

I looked out at the lake. The sun glinted off the water. I shielded my eyes. Big Rideau Lake is huge. I couldn't see past the first narrows, but it stretched for twenty miles or so. Then there were a bunch more lakes before you finally got to Wild Lake. Little Wild Lake. What were the chances Greer Hunter would end up renting there? I had seen the huge A-frame. It stood high on a cliff. In my mind it became a castle. I imagined us — Carrie and me — hand in hand, trembling in a cavernous chamber, the doors barred behind us. There was Greer Hunter, in a midnight-blue cape.

"Welcome," she said. Then she clicked her fingers, and Roger, the Man from Gap, appeared from behind a curtain. "Roger, please show the little girls what we have in store for them."

Roger, smiling like Vanna White, obediently pulled back the curtains to reveal a glittering array of prizes: a CD player, a new guitar, a camera, high-powered binoculars, clothes, shoes, books and a beautiful — *perfect* — laptop computer.

"Well, what have you got for me?"asked Hunter, her teeth gleaming. "Something of Human Interest, I hope. A real Tearjerker."

Like Dorothy meek-and-mild, I stepped forward and told her.

"Rumpelstiltskin!" she screeched, rubbing her hands together with glee. "I love it! And?"

But there was no "and."

Immediately her obscene smile vanished. She snapped her fingers, the curtain closed, and the whole scene vanished.

Maybe the pop guy was right. Maybe I had been getting too much sun.

I put my shoes on, marched up to Main Street and started home. Up ahead I saw Fries' tank parked outside J & W Men's Wear. I waited in a store entranceway, and sure enough, a moment later, out of the jingling door came Fries with clothing boxes under both arms. Mr. Grimm, the tailor, held the door for him, and the two of them shared a laugh on the sidewalk.

A laugh?

It was true. Fries was laughing! And it wasn't just his mouth. His whole face was laughing. His eyes, his nose, his ears, his hair were laughing. His whole body was shaking. It was certifiably creepy.

Still laughing, he climbed into his horrible brown tank and waved goodbye.

"Break a leg," said Mr. Grimm.

Fries revved up his car, which belched oily smoke. Then he set off up Main Street. Main Street curves around the foot of the lake, so I set off running along the sidewalk to see which direction he headed. I must have bumped into a person or two, and I know I banged my shin on someone's bike — I've got the scar to prove it — but I didn't lose sight of him, not until he slowed to make a turn at the edge of town. He turned north up the Lakeshore Road.

◆

When I got home, Carrie had called. A Code Red: phone immediately.

"You're not going to believe this," she said.

So what else was new?

She told me about her trip to the library that afternoon to pick up some stuff for the cottage. She was especially interested in picking up a bird book since we had seen an osprey at the cottage the last time we were up there. We were really hoping to find the nest this time.

"While I was waiting to check the book out, I sort of casually asked the librarian if Fries had a library card.

"'The fellow down at Barb and Bruno's?'" said the librarian. "'Oh, no. Nothing could drag him in here. Not since the big fire.'"

"The big fire?" I said. "What fire?"

"It was before we were born," said Carrie. "The library almost burned to the ground about fifteen years ago."

"And Fries got trapped?" I asked.

"No, that's the amazing part. He never even used the library, but he saw the flames from the pool hall and rushed over."

I grimaced. "Just what you'd expect," I said. I could see him, his eyes all scrinched up, laughing his huge, weird laugh as the library burned to the ground.

"Get this," said Carrie. "He saved somebody's life!"

I was too stunned to speak.

"He just ran into the burning building and carried this girl out. Can you imagine?"

I tried. I saw him in my mind's eye carrying a girl like a gigantic sack of potatoes over his shoulder.

"And that's how he burned his face," I said.

"Yes!" There was a pause. "Don't you get it, Sam? Fries is a hero. We've got our story."

But something was wrong. "It's supposed to be a tragedy," I said. "That's what we told Hunter."

"I've already thought about that," said Carrie. "Listen. Guy saves girl, is disfigured for life, ends up forgotten, slinging fries in a burger stand. Is that a tragedy or what? Sounds like *People Like Us* material to me."

She was right. I could hardly believe it. It was probably something just like that. "This is what he was talking about the other day," I said. "About people minding their own business. He really was a celebrity once. There must have been people prying into his life, wanting to know how it felt, that kind of thing..." Then something else popped into my mind. "Did you get his name?"

"That's the weird thing," said Carrie. "The librarian said he'd been called the Lord of the Fries for so long she couldn't remember. It's not as if he ever comes into the library or anything. But she said I could look it up in the archives. He was in all the papers, Sam, and given a medal and everything. Gordie was getting antsy — his diaper was full — so I told her I'd come back."

My head was spinning. I willed my brain to slow down. "We've got to get some proof," I said. "Hunter will want proof."

Carrie agreed. "Before we leave tomorrow, we'll confront him."

I took a deep breath and nodded. Everything was falling into place.

That evening I found my Rumpelstiltskin book in my little brother's room. Travis has all my old picture books. I sneak in and look them over sometimes. On the page where Rumpelstiltskin was dancing around the fire — the page where he sings his little song and accidentally gives away his name — I discovered a picture I had drawn when I was a kid, a picture of a bird. Actually it might have been a bird or it might have been a rabbit eating a big leaf of lettuce. It was hard to tell.

I settled down on the bed and read the story. Ooh, it made me angry. What a scumbag the prince was. And what a complete dipstick the girl was for marrying him.

"She must have been pretty dim," I said to myself.

Travis came in right about then. "Oh, I know that one," he said. "I like the part where he rips his head off. But there's one thing I don't get."

He held the book open at the page where I had drawn in the margin. "Is this a bird or a rabbit?"

◆

Barb and Bruno's Burger Barn was closed.

We had managed to convince Carrie's parents to stop there on our way out of town. There was a hand-drawn sign in the window. The lights were out. Our hearts sank.

"That's strange," said Carrie's mother. "Closed on a Saturday?"

Shaking his head, Carrie's father put the car back in gear and pulled out onto the street. "You never know these days," he said. "Businesses are closing left and right. I hear big Jack Prince even sold his car franchise and moved out of town."

Carrie and I looked at each other, question marks popping out all over the place. Unfortunately neither of her parents knew exactly why Prince had closed up shop.

We pleaded with her father to let us go to the library, but it didn't open until noon.

"Did you ever find out that fella's name?" Carrie's mother asked. "What did you call him, the Lord of the Fries?"

"Yeah," said Carrie. "His name's Rumpelstilt-skin."

"Ah," said Carrie's mother. "Well, then he's not from around here. That's not a local name."

They had a good laugh about that, but Carrie and I flashed each other looks of dread. Barb and

Bruno's closed. Jack Prince gone. The plot was getting thicker and juicier and here we were leaving town with next to nothing.

"Some investigative journalists we turned out to be," I said.

"Hey," said Carrie, "I'd say we've done just fine. We'll ask Hunter for a bit more time."

That made me nervous. She had said there was good money in it. Very good money. And it was a great story, better even than we could have imagined. But something I couldn't quite put my finger on made me squeamish. I tried to push Greer Hunter from my mind.

Gordie helped. He was strapped into his car seat between us. We were having a good time fussing over him and dangling stuff for him to grab with his tiny perfect fingers.

For some reason it made me think of Rumpelstiltskin, the deal the princess cut with him to give him her firstborn child. I mentioned it to Carrie.

"I guess you'd do whatever you had to if you were going to get your head chopped off in the morning," she said.

I agreed. "And it's not as if she'd actually had the baby yet," I added.

Then Gordie hit himself in the head with his rattle, startling himself. We laughed and oohed and ahhhed and kissed his little head.

"But could you imagine," said Carrie, "when the Rumpster comes to actually claim the baby?"

"Yeah. You'd do anything to keep it."

I looked at Gordie. You couldn't just give up

something like a baby without a fight. But I still felt sort of sorry for Rumpelstiltskin. He was cheated.

Gordie fell asleep, and Carrie dug out the book on ospreys. I looked out my window at the scenery. It was so beautiful.

I looked over at Carrie. She had her window open a smidge, and the wind was blowing her hair in a swirl around her face. She was smiling happily, not reading. I knew what she was thinking about. Fame and fortune.

"Carrie?" I said. "What about our promise?"

"What promise?"

"To Fries. That we wouldn't tell another living soul his name."

"No problem," she said. "He didn't tell us his real name. So the deal is off. Right? When we get back, we'll dig out the stuff from the archives, and we'll be all set."

I looked out the window. "There might be a catch," I said. "What if his name really is Rumpelstiltskin?"

•

We got to the cottage and, like magic, we forgot all about the Lord of the Fries and Greer Hunter and *People Like Us*. We got our swim stuff, sun hats, about a ton of zinc ointment, got out the boat, grabbed life jackets, a thermos of lemonade, a year's supply of granola bars and the binoculars, and headed out on Solitude Bay.

It was so quiet. So peaceful. It was the kind of place where seeing a big bird might just be enough to make a person truly happy.

We saw the osprey right away, circling the end of

the bay. We each got a good long turn with the binoculars, watching it glide on the wind, hardly flapping at all. It looked like a bald eagle wearing a black mask. It looked as if it were getting ready to dive as soon as it saw just the right fish. We'd never seen it do that — dive, I mean. Maybe today.

Suddenly a car horn started honking. The honking didn't stop. Then there were more cars honking. We couldn't see them through the trees, but they were on the Old Wild Lake Road. It sounded like a traffic jam, which was ridiculous; we were in the middle of nowhere.

Honk, honk, honk.

The parade of cars was fading as they headed towards Picnic Point at the northern tip of the lake, but by now the damage was done. The honking had driven off the osprey.

We waited and waited for it to return. The sun was hot, so we rowed towards shore to get in the shade. We swam off the boat a bit and waited. And waited.

"Listen," said Carrie. She had brought the library book and was reading from it. "The osprey is monotypic. You know what that means?"

"Is it like monotonous?" I asked.

"No, it means they are the only bird in their family."

"Small family."

Carrie was shaking her head. "This is amazing. There's only one species of osprey in the whole world. I guess you'd say 'specie' in that case. I've never heard of such a thing. I mean there are two hundred and ninety *thousand* species of beetle in the world." Carrie knows things like this. "There's twenty-seven thousand species of beetles in North America alone," she said. "How can there be only one specie of osprey?"

I had heard the speedboat even before she started speaking. The sound of the motor had grown all the time she had been going on about beetles. I couldn't see it yet, because Solitude Bay has a narrow opening, but it was definitely coming our way. First a motorcade, now speedboats. Our osprey wasn't likely to come back this way any too soon.

Just as Carrie was finishing her little rant, telling me how many kinds of ants there were, the boat appeared, flashing across the mouth of the bay. I trained the binoculars on it.

There were four people in the big outboard, and everyone seemed dressed up. Two girls in fancy dresses with flowers in their windblown hair. Two guys wearing bow ties and frilly shirts. There was someone water-skiing behind the boat. I followed the rope with my eyes.

"Holy stinkweed!"

"What is it?"

"It is *definitely* monotypic!" I said.

"Is that guy really wearing a tuxedo?"

I was shaking with excitement as I handed Carrie the binocs and turned in my seat to fire up our little seven horsepower. "Take a look," I said.

The sputter of the putt-putt coming to life almost covered her yowl of surprise. "Quick! Don't lose them," she said.

All thoughts of osprey in action vanished from our minds. The water-skier in the tuxedo was none other than the Lord of the Fries.

There was no chance of actually catching the souped-up ski boat, but we chugged out into the lake far enough to see where it finally landed. By then Fries had dropped off one of his skis and done a slalom circuit of the lake. He was amazing. Finally he landed right at the dock — right *on* the dock! Probably didn't even get his cuffs wet. There was a crowd to greet him when he landed.

"This is totally bonkers!" cried Carrie.

Speechless, she handed me the binoculars. I turned the little knob to focus the happy group on the dock, all dressed in powder blue and pink and peach, almost as if it were a —

"Good grief!"

There was a big woman in a white gown kissing him. Kissing the Lord of the Fries.

I cut the motor. We sat, Carrie and I, just letting the waves lap against the side of the boat. Then Carrie took the binocs from me. She trained them on the dock where the speedboat had landed. I watched her scan the shore. I knew what she was thinking as soon as she looked at me. Her eyes were full of lakeshine.

"I know Hunter wanted a tragedy. But I bet you she'll pay us even more for a tragedy with a happy ending."

I was already revving up the motor.

We raced — hah! chugged — back to the cottage. We changed and grabbed our bikes. That's when Carrie's mom called us back. We had to look after Gordie for a couple of hours. We had promised. There was no way out.

So it was not until after supper that we could get

away. It was a long way around the lake, with lots of hills. Who knew if the wedding party would still be there? We stopped on the hill above the marina where we could see down the lake. It was dusk. There seemed to be bonfires at Picnic Point.

By the time we rounded the lake it was almost sunset. We knew we must be close, because there were cars parked all along the road.

Someone was playing a fiddle; people were dancing. Kids were running around sneaking drinks out of grown-ups' glasses. Through the trees we saw glimpses of powder blue, pink and peach whirling around. There were lanterns hung in the trees. It looked like fairyland.

And there, amid the trees, Fries' awful brown tank was parked in a dirt driveway beside the sweetest fairy-tale log cabin.

Carrie grabbed my arm so tightly I almost fell off my bike. "We should have brought my dad's camera," she said.

Why hadn't we thought of that? *People Like Us* always had juicy photos. I stopped and looked back up the road. There was no way. It would be dark by the time we got back.

We ditched our bikes, walked along a bit. We looked out of place, but nobody seemed to mind. We overheard someone say how nice the wedding had been. We tried to imagine it.

"Do you, Lord of the Fries, take this woman to be your lawful wedded wife?"

"Yeah, yeah, yeah."

We saw Barb and Bruno in fancy duds and Constable Giroux playing the guitar. We steered ourselves clear of them, down towards the lake. Then we saw him. Fries. He was sitting on a log beside a fire on the beach. A bunch of folks were sitting around in a circle, including his bride, who sat in a deck chair still in her wedding dress, Fries' rented tuxedo jacket around her shoulders. Her blonde hair was all piled up in an elaborate bouffant, but it was coming undone around the edges. She looked pretty in her fluffy, puffy wedding gown.

"Like a sundae," I said. And that's when I knew where I had seen her before. "It's the woman who works at the Dairy Queen," I whispered to Carrie. "Daisy Miller."

Carrie gasped. "She must have been there that day Fries beat up on Jack Prince."

I nodded excitedly. "Probably in the back smooching with Fries." We both shuddered with disgust.

But our curiosity was burning, so we moved in close. The brush was thick, but finally we found a spot almost directly above the fire.

Daisy had taken off her shoes. A little boy was burying her bare feet in the sand with a shovel. Every now and then she'd pop one chubby toe out and the boy would giggle. Then he'd bury her feet again.

"Hey, BoBo," said Fries, tickling the kid behind the neck. He giggled even more.

Daisy reached out to Fries and patted him affectionately on the knee. Oh, what a smile was on his face. It transformed him. All the meanness seemed to drain right out of him. His eyes sparkled. His poor cooked cheek looked like what it really was: the mark of a hero.

Then he kissed her hand! Everybody made a fuss about that. The bride blushed.

"Does this make Daisy the Lady of the Fries?" I whispered.

Carrie thought for a moment. "How about the Lady of the Shakes?" I liked that.

And then someone spoke to Fries and called him by name.

We had his name!

Now we had everything we needed. Well, almost. Oh, for a camera! How would we ever convince Greer Hunter this fairy-tale wedding had really happened without some pictures?

We stayed at the wedding until the mosquitoes came out. By floating around the edges of the party, where Fries couldn't see us, and eavesdropping like good investigative journalists, we put the whole amazing story together. It was, of course, Daisy Fries had rescued from the fire. And he was there again for her years later to pick up the pieces when her marriage to Jack Prince fell apart. Jack had been cruel. Fries had always carried a torch for her. He had been her knight in shining armour.

"Her newt in shining armour," I whispered to Carrie. She laughed, but I was sorry I'd said it. He didn't seem so newtish anymore.

The breakup with Jack Prince had received a lot of publicity, it seemed. Daisy had been plagued by the press.

"Of course, Fries knows all about the paparazzi," said someone. "What he had to go through after the fire, poor devil."

"You can say that again. Remember that headline alongside a close-up of his scarred face: A FREAK FOR LOVE."

"They pursued him to Hell-and-Gone."

To Hell-and-Gone, I thought, as Carrie and I collected our bikes and headed home. It sounded like a lonely place.

◆

The next morning, bright and early, we pushed off from Carrie's dock and headed at putt-putt pace around the lake towards our date with destiny. Our route took us via Picnic Point. This time we had Carrie's dad's camera complete with zoom lens. We didn't really expect to see anyone around, but we wanted something to show Hunter, even if it was only the Just Married sign on the back of Fries' junker.

We weren't sure if we were actually supposed to compose the story for *People Like Us* just yet. We figured not. So we had written it all out point by point the night before. Even in point form it was truly astonishing.

Over the sound of the motor Carrie said, almost solemnly, "I think I'm going to put my share of the money into my university savings account." This was a big change from a vacation in Florida and a back-to-school shopping spree.

As we suspected, Picnic Point was empty of cars and with only the odd balloon caught in the trees to show that there had been a wedding bash the night before.

We saw the little house. With the morning sun glancing through the woods it looked truly magical. Carrie cut the motor and focussed the camera. Click. Click.

She got the sign on the car, too.

We drifted. How silent it was after the festivities of the night before. There was only the creaking of the boat, the lapping of the waves, and laughter...

Laughter?

I picked up the binoculars. "There!" I whispered.

It was too good to be true. There was the happy couple walking along the road hand in hand. She was still in her wedding gown, he in his tux.

Click. Click. Click.

Carrie zoomed in and took picture after picture: Fries picking a flower with his toes, Daisy twirling around...

"Beauty!" whispered Carrie.

They were on the beach now. Shoeless and sockless and wading through the surf, she holding her skirts up high.

Click. Click.

"They don't seem to have seen us," I said. I prayed they wouldn't. I felt like such a sneak.

At last the agony was over. The camera whirred, the back popped open and Carrie took out the roll of film, which she placed in its protective canister. "Can you believe it?" she said as she stuffed the canister securely in her pocket.

"No," I said. I must have sounded as glum as I felt, because Carrie looked at me and frowned.

She placed the camera in a waterproof bag and started the motor. Now they saw us. I saw Fries gazing our way, shielding his eyes from the sun and shaking his fist. We were probably too far out for him to recognize. I hoped so.

As we headed down the eastern shore towards

Dortchen Point, I played the snapshots through in my mind. Carrie was pretty good with a camera; with any luck she had captured some first-class stolen moments. I looked at her. Her eyes were on our destination. I turned to see it looming ahead, the morning light turning the huge windows of the A-frame to burnished steel.

There would be more pictures, of course. Professional pictures. Fries growling through his window down at the Burger Barn, dandling BoBo on his knee, water-skiing in his rented tux. If he thought he was hounded after the fire, wait until *People Like Us* got hold of him!

Carrie must have been reading my mind. "You never know, he may enjoy the publicity," she said. "I mean, it's not like before — after the fire. This time the lord has got his lady."

I snuffled in a kind of disgruntled way.

"Hey!" said Carrie. "I bet they'll get some money out of it, too. They could start their own business. Wouldn't that be great?"

I hadn't thought of that. To judge by the look of Fries' car, they could do with some cash. That's when I got the idea of what I would do with my money. I'd give it to Fries and his new bride. Well, part of it anyway. The idea helped ease my conscience. Well, part of it anyway.

I turned in my seat. There was someone on the deck of the A-frame. It was Hunter. The sun lit up her red hair; it seemed to shoot out from her head like flames. She raised a pair of binoculars to her eyes. She got us in her sights. Soon we would climb the long, steep stairs up to the clifftop. I could imagine us, out of breath, telling our story, her not believing it because it was too good, saying we had made it all up, and that was when Carrie would triumphantly hand her the precious roll of film. Our proof. I could imagine her smiling down at it in her hand and then closing her fingers around it, making a fist, squeezing it tighter and tighter until the happy pictures inside dripped out onto the deck, one by one, like blood.

What was I thinking? There's such a thing as having too good an imagination. But the cold, hard truth had never felt so cold or hard.

I turned to Carrie. She had a steady grip on the throttle of the motor, her other hand grasping the gunwale just as tightly. Her hair was flying; her face was speckled with spray. She fixed me in her gaze. She looked grim. But as I watched, her eyebrows slid towards each other. In her eyes I saw my own face. I had to say something, now or never.

I was just about to when her glance slithered away from mine and her eyes looked up, up, up into the summer morning sky.

It was flying all alone, one of a kind. The osprey.

Carrie shut the motor. The boat rose on its own flood and stopped. She stood up in the rocking boat and pointed, soundlessly, but I had already seen it circling. My eyes flickered away for just a moment towards the cliff. Greer Hunter had seen the bird as well. She was following it with her binoculars.

Carrie cupped her hands. "Hey!" she yelled.

At first I thought she was yelling at Greer Hunter, telling her to mind her own business, that it was our osprey! But it was the osprey Carrie was yelling at.

"Hey, bird!" she yelled. "Want a prize?" Then from her pocket she drew out the little black canister. She looked at me as she yanked the film out of it. Her eyes were wide and kind of crazy. She held the film so that I could see it, so that there was no doubt in my mind what she was thinking. What she was going to do.

Yes! I nodded. Do it. Do it!

Then with all her might she hurled the film into the sky. We watched it rise, end over end, in a lazy arc and fall with gathering momentum into the lake — splash!

That's when the osprey dove.

It pulled in its wings and seemed almost to drop out of the sky, plummeting towards the shining surface of the lake. Pow! Then it was rising again, something shining in its claws. Gleaming in the sun like stolen gold.

ICK

Garnet and Brody were going swimming. Brody directed Garnet to the cupboard where the beach towels were kept while he raided the kitchen for pop and taco chips. In the bottom of the linen cupboard Garnet found a tin of fish food and a little pamphlet entitled *Goldfish Are Easy to Care For*.

"I didn't know you had goldfish."

"That's all that's left of them," said Brody.

Garnet thumbed through the pamphlet. "Not so easy to care for after all, huh?" There was a drawing of a goldfish. "This guy looks pretty chipper."

Brody looked at the page. "Yeah, I guess. For a goldfish."

"What happened, Brody? Cat get them?"

"Nope," said Brody. "Ick."

"Ick?"

"That's what it's called. They start getting these white spots on their gills and fins, and then they just get gross and float to the surface."

"Ick!"

"Right."

Garnet put the pamphlet back in the cupboard, holding it gingerly by one corner, as if there might be some Ick left on it. He gathered up a couple of towels.

"Great name for a disease."

"Yeah," said Brody as they headed out into the blistering sun. They wheeled off down the drive and south on Boardwalk towards the lake.

In his mind's eye Garnet could see the goldfish flipping over and floating to the top of the tank. "I mean, there are terrible diseases out there, like Hodgkin's disease or Parkinson's disease. They don't sound so bad. But Ick...what causes it?" Garnet sounded worried, as if maybe a person could catch it.

"Not flossing properly," said Brody. "How should I know?"

"They were your fish," said Garnet.

♦

The lake was freezing. It was still early in June. Randy and some of the other guys were already out on the raft, pushing each other off, playing ragtag with somebody's balled-up Hawaiian shirt. They waved at Brody and Garnet, yelled at them to come out. There was nothing for it but to dive right in or look chicken. Brody stripped off his shirt and jumped. He had some flesh on him. But Garnet thought twice about it. Thinking twice was one of the things he did best. He was skinny. Athletic guys like Randy tended to tease him. And there was always the chance that some girls might show up.

He decided to keep his T-shirt on. He didn't want any girl counting his ribs.

As soon as he climbed the ladder onto the raft, a balled-up, sopping-wet Hawaiian shirt ploughed him in the face.

"Gar's it!" yelled Randy, and then he cannonballed into the water right beside the ladder. Popeye did the same and Mulligan and Ace. Brody gave Garnet a hand up, then pushed him back into the water. It was summer, at last.

The game went on like that for a while, and then they all lay around on the raft breathing hard and letting the sun scorch the gooseflesh off their snow-white carcasses.

Garnet was the last one still shivering. He kept looking up, leaning on his elbows, surveying the scene. The breeze was fresh.

"What are you so nervous about?" said Randy.

Garnet wasn't really nervous. He just didn't want to miss stuff. So while the others roasted, Garnet freeze-dried in the breeze. He looked down at his fingers. They were white with cold.

"Ick! I got Ick!"

Then he and Brody had to explain about Ick to everybody. Soon they all had it, and everybody was pulling faces, falling over and rolling off the raft into the water, dead. Until some girls came — Becky and Sal and Sal's cousin from the city. Then everybody forgot about Ick.

◆

Garnet didn't think about it again until the fall, a week after school started, the day they transferred him to the bright class.

"It must have been that project you did last year on Chernobyl," said Brody when they were walking home from school. "I told you it was way too good."

"Well, I'm not staying," grumped Garnet. "I don't feel good in there with people like Becky

Goodhue and Danny Berubian and that crowd."

"What about Annaliese DeLillo-Dorrel?" said Brody, stretching out her already dramatic name to an absurd length.

Garnet worked at keeping his composure. "Annaliese possesses qualities of unusual delicacy and craftsmanship," he said.

"Hello?"

"It's the definition of *exquisite*. I looked it up."

"Well, if you want to get out of the bright class, you'd better cut out that looking-up stuff right now."

Garnet punched him a few times, but his heart wasn't in it. He really didn't feel that he was in the same league as his new classmates. He was good at thinking twice; it took him twice as long to get an answer. But the experts had other ideas. He was a lateral thinker, according to them. "Like a crab?" he said. The principal, Ms. McGregor, and the enrichment teacher, Mr. Suhanic, smiled knowingly at each other.

"And the worst thing," said Garnet, "is that this is supposed to be some kind of reward for being smart. 'Hey, Garnet! Good for you. You're so smart we're gonna give you *tons* more homework.'"

Brody laughed. "No, I know what it was. It was that story you wrote for Clairborne. What was it called?"

"'The Sneaking Hunch and the Wink of a Nye,'" said Garnet unhappily. It had been a great story. It had won a prize. How was he supposed to know it would betray him like this?

"Yeah, that was it," said Brody. "It was brilliant.

What was the Hunch called?"

"Bucket," said Garnet.

"Yeah," said Brody fondly. "Bucket the Hunch. He was so cool. And the little guy…"

"Max the Nye."

"That was it. Brilliant!"

"Tell me, Brody," said Garnet. "Do you remember anything about the story at all?"

Brody thought for a long, drawn-out moment. "What story?" he said. Then he winked. "Nobody's puttin' me in no bright class."

Garnet rubbed his head. He had a new buzz cut for school, and he tended to rub it when he was thinking. His dad said he looked like Aladdin rubbing the magic lamp.

"It's like Ick," said Garnet.

"Hello?"

Garnet shrugged. "Remember? Like the goldfish you had."

Brody made a meal out of trying to remember. "Oh, yeah," he said. He thought a bit. "So are you saying they should have slowly lowered you into the bright class in a plastic bag?"

"What are you talking about?"

Brody kicked a stone that skittered ahead of them down the sidewalk. He kept his eye on it; he had plans for that stone. "It's what we were supposed to do with the goldfish when we brought them home from the pet shop. Let the water in their bag get to the same temperature as the aquarium by lowering them in their bag into the water. Get them used to it."

Garnet tried to imagine himself sitting in the

bright class in a bag of water. Brody let fly at his chosen stone. It skipped all the way to Garnet's driveway. The boys joined it there, looked down at it.

Garnet thought about inviting Brody in, then remembered the assignment he had to do on the North American Free Trade Agreement. Things he used to overhear on the news — now he had to write assignments on them! It wasn't fair. He sighed and headed up the lane to his house. Brody called after him. "Better take a good long look at your fins tonight, Gar."

Garnet made a sickly expression and waved his arms around in a watery way.

◆

Being in the bright class was a bit like being in an aquarium. There were always people coming in to take a look at the colourful creatures swimming around in there, to teach them something enriching. A calligrapher came in and showed them how to do Chinese writing. A test pilot talked about travelling at Mach speed. A politician even dropped by to explain the government's new policy on education. They all beamed at the class as if they were the calligraphers and pilots and politicians of tomorrow. Sometimes they even said things like that. Garnet didn't like all the attention. He scuttled like a crab out of the light.

To amuse himself, he started trying to categorize his new aquarium mates.

Danny Berubian was the class piranha. He was viciously smart. He attacked information as if it were something that might get away unless he devoured it immediately. He almost tore the leg off the visiting politician.

Maurice Graves was more like a blowfish. He was all puffed up with intelligence, and he kept his mouth shut in case any of it leaked out. He leaned over tests guardedly, his face down close to the surface of his desk, looking suspiciously from left to right in case anyone was copying.

Garnet actually wrote that on a test. He didn't say it was Danny or Maurice. He spent the whole period observing and describing the kids in the class as they wrote the test, as if they were fish. The test was on the five senses. Garnet didn't answer a single question. He was hoping maybe it would get him transferred. But Mr. Suhanic gave him an A+ instead. That was the trouble with being in the bright class.

In his rebellious moment he even dared describe the exquisite Annaliese DeLillo-Dorrel as an angelfish, refined and fastidious. She had luxuriant red hair, which streamed out behind her. Actually her hair was auburn. He had looked through his mother's art books until he found hair the same colour and then he'd asked his mother what the proper name for such a colour might be. Just in case he was still in the bright class in February and he wanted to send someone a Valentine's card.

Annaliese glided through Garnet's thoughts the way she did through the enrichment program, with her pale blue eyes on high beam. English, math, geography — it was all equally wonderful. Everything was worth knowing; everything was a pink coral reef of delight. She even made Garnet, the crab, feel as if he might be worth knowing.

He asked her if she wanted to tag along with him and Brody on their way home.

"That would be wonderful," she said.

Brody met them in the yard. "So what'd you guys do today?" he said. "Did Albert Einstein come in and do some math with you?"

Annaliese gave Brody one of her angelfish smiles. "Einstein's dead," she said.

"Get out," said Brody.

"It's true. He died in 1955."

"Don't mind him," said Garnet.

"Oh, all right," said Annaliese cheerily.

And she didn't. She didn't say another word until they reached her turnoff. She didn't act superior or anything. In fact, she seemed to listen intently to the boys' chatter the whole time. She even laughed once.

At Thorncliffe Hill Road she said goodbye in a delighted voice, her eyes shining. "See you in class, Garnet," she said. "Nice to meet you, Brody." Then she headed up to where the big houses were, over-looking the ravine, while Garnet and Brody headed down Boardwalk into the valley of little houses.

"Is she always that boisterous?" said Brody when they were out of earshot. Then he roared with laughter.

Garnet punched him a few times, afraid Annaliese might hear them and mistake his laughter for ridicule. But would ridicule bother her? Nothing seemed to.

Boisterous was a Clairborne word from when Brody and Garnet had been classmates. "Boys, are we being a tad boisterous?" Clairborne used to say. Brody had been sure it was spelled boysterous — whoever heard of girlsterous? — until Garnet showed it to him in a dictionary.

Garnet rubbed his closely cropped head. He stared up through the trees, caught a glimpse of Annaliese in her blue and yellow coat, then lost her again.

"I have a theory," he said. "She doesn't really say anything much unless you actually ask her something."

Brody looked hard at Garnet. "Weird," he said.

"No, Brody. It's called shy."

◆

Annaliese seemed to get along with everybody, but as far as Garnet could tell, she didn't have any close friends. Garnet and Brody were happy to take on the job. The three of them took to walking home together. Every journey began with a question from Brody. "So what'd you do today? Build an atomic reactor?" or "Is it true that the whole bright class is going to Chechnya on a fact-finding mission?"

Annaliese always answered his question. Brody would ask her to laugh whenever he said something funny, and she always did.

Then, after they had parted ways at Thorncliffe Hill, Brody always had a question or two for Garnet. "What drug do you think she's on?" or "What planet do you think she's really from?"

It was obvious he was smitten with Annaliese DeLillo-Dorrel. So was Garnet. She was a beautiful mystery.

◆

Then the rains of October rolled around, and Mr. Suhanic left the enrichment program all of a sudden to become a vice-principal in another school. Everybody was sad to see him go.

His replacement couldn't have been more of a contrast. Suhanic had been middle-aged and rumpled. I. C. Bellamy was young and snazzy.

"He had a master's degree by the time he was twenty," said Annaliese. "Isn't that wonderful?"

"He presses his Levi's," said Garnet.

"He actually met Andrew Lloyd Webber," said Annaliese.

"And his hair," said Garnet.

"He met Andrew Lloyd Webber's hair?" said Brody.

"No," said Garnet. "I meant he presses his hair."

"He is very neat," said Annaliese.

"He's a shark," muttered Garnet under his breath. He managed to change the topic, but as soon as the boys dropped Annaliese off at Thorncliffe Hill, Garnet filled in Brody on the new teacher. "He calls us the brightketeers."

Brody smacked his palm to his forehead. "Ay-yi-yi. That bad, eh?"

"Worse. The girls have gone gaga over him."

"So I noticed."

They walked along silently in the drizzle until a car speeding by splashed them.

"Bet that was him!" said Garnet, wiping the mud off his sleeve and pants leg.

"Does he drive a red Mustang with SX APL on the license plate?"

Garnet looked glum. "Probably."

◆

I. C. Bellamy did not drive a red Mustang. He drove a cute little black Jeep with cute yellow pinstripes. And he didn't have vanity plates. "As if he could be any more vain than he already is," said Garnet.

He decided that if Bellamy was a shark, at least he wasn't a great white or a hammerhead. More like a leopard shark. Not truly deadly, just sneaky. He didn't want to talk about Bellamy, and he certainly didn't want to talk about the change that had come over Annaliese. Brody did. Especially when she didn't join them on the walk home one night.

"He picked Annaliese for the math team," Garnet explained. "She has to stay after school."

"Oh," said Brody, "that explains the lipstick and eye gunk." He batted his eyes a few times. "Oh, Mr. Bellamy," he said in a high-pitched voice. "Is it true that I. C. stands for irresistibly cute?"

It was Brody's idea to slip around the back of the school and take a peek at what the math club was up to. Garnet didn't like the idea but followed along. There was Bellamy, his sweater draped casually over his shoulders, one leg thrown casually over the edge of his desk.

"His penny loafers are blinding," said Brody, shielding his eyes.

"He puts quarters in them," said Garnet.

The math team was crowded into the desks nearest the teacher. They were hanging on his every word. He was pointing at some problem on the blackboard. His eyes buzzed. He must have asked a question because suddenly Annaliese's hand shot up. She spoke. Bellamy clapped and handed her the chalk to correct the error on the board.

"Let's get out of here," said Garnet.

But Brody clung to the windowsill. "Funny how the whole math team is girls, huh?"

Garnet tugged at Brody's coat sleeve. Too late. Returning from the board, Annaliese saw them. Her face coloured. She looked down. The boys ducked and ran.

"Guess who feels fourteen years old," said Garnet.

"Garnet," said Brody, a little out of breath from trying to keep up with his friend, "you *are* fourteen."

Garnet only pretended to go in when they passed his place. As soon as Brody had gone around the corner, he headed back up to the junction of Broadway and Thorncliffe Hill Road, where he waited in the growing dark for Annaliese.

The Jeep caught him by surprise. Luckily it had to wait for a passing car before it could turn up Thorncliffe. Garnet had just enough time to jump into the bushes beside the road. He hoped Bellamy hadn't seen him.

Or his only passenger, Annaliese DeLillo-Dorrel.

♦

But Annaliese *had* seen him, both at the class window and at the corner of Thorncliffe. She did not think it was wonderful that he had been spying on her. She did not think it was wonderful that he was concerned.

"He was driving me home because it was dark," she said, her pale blue eyes flashing. "That's what gentlemen do."

Garnet had never seen her angry before.

"I didn't know she had it in her," said Brody when he heard about it the next day. They were walking home alone again. The rain had let up, but it was grey and cold. Garnet dug his hands deeper into his jacket pockets.

"It got worse," he said. "I tried to explain to her about Bellamy being a shark, and she said I had a dirty mind."

Brody shook his head, put his arm around Garnet's shoulder. "I'm gonna miss her," he said. "She was the best audience I ever had. Well, the most obedient audience I ever had. You tell her to laugh, she laughs. You can't beat that."

Garnet didn't answer. He was thinking hard. Thinking twice.

When he got home, he tried to do his homework, but he couldn't concentrate on global warming. He went outside and dug his bike out of the shed. There were cobwebs on it, and dead flies. He had moth-balled it for winter weeks ago, but he had to do something, go somewhere.

He headed down Boardwalk towards the lake. He pumped his way up Lighthouse Hill and skidded out, scraping his hand on the gravel. He pushed his bike to the top of the hill, climbed back on board and hurled himself forward again. His hands were freezing. He should have worn gloves. He pedalled harder, having to turn his head away from the bitter wind off the lake. He should have worn his helmet.

He arrived at last at the stretch of beach where they swam in summer. The diving raft was pulled up high on the rocky shore. He sat on the edge of it, breathing hard, clammy with sweat. The pulse in his cut hand was beating painfully. He was bleeding. He looked for somewhere to wipe it and saw a frozen clump of material on the beach. It turned out to be the Hawaiian shirt they had played ragtag with all summer. Now it was rock hard and gave only slightly when he pressed his bleeding palm against it.

What was the use, he thought, of being a lateral thinker when every which way his thoughts took him led to only one place, only one person?

The sun was being swallowed up earlier every day. Garnet rode the last bit of the way back in the dark. He arrived home to the bustle of supper preparation, his mother straining pasta and his father tossing salad, singing along to one of his geezer tapes, the Stones singing "Get Off of My Cloud." He arrived home to find that Annaliese had phoned.

He called her back immediately.

"I'm sorry," she said.

"No, I'm the one who's sorry."

"You don't understand."

"It doesn't matter if I understand," said Garnet. "It's none of my business."

Annaliese didn't speak right away. Her breathing sounded funny. Suddenly Garnet realized she had been crying.

"Are you all right?"

She sniffed. "Yes."

"What happened?"

"I guess I just liked the attention," she said. "I didn't really think it was anything serious."

"What'd he do?"

"Nothing. Nothing really. He drove me home again. He said he really likes me. I'm just...I don't know. I'm scared. What am I going to do?"

Garnet plugged his ear. It was hard to concentrate with the Stones blaring in the background.

"I'll think of something," he said. "Don't worry."

Annaliese sniffed again. Blew her nose. "I feel pretty stupid," she said.

"I know the feeling," said Garnet.

♦

The next day he and Brody made sure they were in the parking lot of the school just when the math team meeting broke up. They saw Bellamy and Annaliese walking towards his Jeep. He was carrying her backpack. His other hand was at her elbow, guiding her along. A real gentleman. She was looking for the boys. She waved when she saw them. They waved back.

Brody called to her. "We're just on our way home. Care to join us?"

Annaliese shrugged shyly. "Sure. Thanks."

"I don't know about this," said Bellamy, his free hand on his hip. He was grinning, shaking his head. "You sure these dudes can be trusted?"

"We'll get her straight home, sir," said Garnet. He tried to keep his voice light. He almost succeeded.

"It's your call, Miss DeLillo-Dorrel," said Bellamy, bowing gallantly. Then he held up his hand, palm up. "Hope the rain holds off." He tipped his head towards the Jeep.

Annaliese, avoiding his eyes, took her backpack from him and pulled a compact umbrella out of it.

"You are amazing," he said, his eyes all twinkly. "Okay, kids, see you tomorrow."

They watched him climb into his Jeep and wheel out of the parking lot. As soon as he was out of sight, Annaliese sighed with relief. "Thanks," she said, her voice wavering a little.

"Oh, you are just so amazing," said Brody, trying to make his voice all twinkly. Annaliese didn't respond. "You can laugh," said Brody. She tried, not very successfully.

♦

It was late when Annaliese phoned. She apologized. Garnet said he was still up, but a sleepy yawn betrayed him. He was soon wide awake, however. Bellamy had called her.

"He had some information for me," she said. "But it was nothing that couldn't have waited until tomorrow. We talked a bit. My folks were out, and he said if I needed a baby-sitter, he'd be happy to come over. He said he was joking, but it didn't sound like joking, if you know what I mean."

"I know what you mean," said Garnet. "Are you scared?"

She thought a moment. "A little. But it's different. When I phoned you yesterday, I was scared because I still wanted him to like me. Now I'm scared because he's creepy."

And persistent, thought Garnet.

"I guess he didn't get the message this afternoon," said Annaliese.

Garnet's mind was hard at work. Too hard. He shook his head to loosen things up, get the fog out. That's when the little crab crawled out sideways from who knows where with an answer in its claw. "Yes!"

"Garnet, what are you laughing about?"

"Mr. I. C. Bellamy," he said. "He's going to wish he hadn't messed around with a class full of brightketeers."

◆

Garnet lay awake for a long time. In the morning light his idea seemed pretty lame. He phoned Brody to run it by him.

"Brilliant!" said Brody. "Wish I could be there to see it."

His faith restored, Garnet phoned Danny Berubian. Danny snapped up the idea in a flash. He even offered to help with the phoning. So, with Annaliese phoning the girls, the word spread to all of the enriched class. The interesting thing was, it didn't take much to persuade them.

"Everyone seemed to know what was going on," said Annaliese. "Everyone but me." She sounded disappointed in herself. "And I'm supposed to be so smart."

"You are," said Garnet. "It's just that you swam a little too far out from the reef."

The classmates worked quickly and smoothly. Before the bell rang, they were ready and in their seats, their hands folded on their desks, waiting. Mr. Bellamy looked impressed.

"Well, well, well. Aren't we all bright-eyed and bushy-tailed?" he said. His twinkly gaze took in everyone, left no one out. But it came to rest on Annaliese. It was only then that he noticed something was different, and his handsome forehead wrinkled.

"Annaliese?" he said.

He walked down the aisle to her desk. He reached out to touch her face, then drew back. There was a white patch on her cheek, no larger than a quarter. With her fingers she brushed back her hair to reveal another white patch on her right earlobe. Dead white.

Maurice Graves, who sat next to Annaliese, spoke up. "It's okay, sir. It's not all that contagious." Maurice's nose was white. So was the back of one of his hands.

Garnet stood up. Half his skull was white. "It's called Ick," he said. "We've all got it. But like Maury said, you don't have to worry. Only kids are susceptible."

Bellamy backed up a step. He glanced around the classroom, seeing what he had not seen when he only had eyes for Annaliese. Everyone was spotted.

"It's stress-related," said Becky Goodhue.

"Maybe you've forgotten how stressful it is being fourteen," said Danny Berubian.

Bellamy was ashen. He stared at Annaliese in disbelief. "Is this your idea of a joke?"

Annaliese averted her eyes.

Even from the next-to-last desk, Garnet could tell she was terrified. He leaped up again. "It's not a joke, sir. It's Ick."

From behind him, where he had been hunched over to avoid being seen, Brody's face rose up, ghostly white, smiling devilishly.

"What are you doing here?" Bellamy demanded.

"We've been quarantined," said Brody. "All the infected ones have to stay together in this room."

Annaliese dared turn around and smile nervously. Garnet intercepted the smile and shared it — fifty-fifty — with his friend.

But Bellamy was not smiling. He strode to the front of the class, swung around and glared at

Brody and Garnet. There was no humour in his eyes. "This is sad," he said. "Pathetic." His gaze flitted back to Annaliese. He shook his head, looked hurt. "From a class like this, I expected a lot more."

Then Annaliese spoke up, her terror overcome. "That's what I was afraid of," she said.

◆

Somebody said he was teaching in a private boys' school in Rwanda. Somebody said they saw him on *America's Most Wanted*. Somebody swore they saw the cute little black Jeep smashed to a pulp at the bottom of Franklin Gorge. Somebody else said they saw the wreck up close, and it was speckled white, the first reported case of automotive Ick.

Garnet just figured I. C. Bellamy had swum back out to the deep, where he belonged.

But the rumours died down pretty quickly when, after three days' absence, he returned.

As soon as the bell rang, he closed the door and stood before the class, his hands folded meekly in front of him.

"I would like to apologize," he said.

You could have heard a snake drop.

"Apparently none of you has reported my conduct to the principal. I owe you for that. It would be within your rights." He looked pale. Took a deep, shaky breath. To Garnet, the performance looked rehearsed, but all the same, it didn't look like acting. Bellamy was genuinely scared.

"I'd like another chance," he said. He bit his lip. "I know I will have to win back your respect. I understand that." He looked around, and his eyes landed at last on Annaliese. Everyone turned to see what she would say.

Garnet hoped that whatever it was, she would take her time. He wanted to see Bellamy squirm on the hook. He wasn't any too sure a leopard shark could change its spots so quickly.

Annaliese's face was red. She looked down at her desktop.

"You don't have to say anything right now," said Bellamy. "I have no right to put you on the spot like this."

Annaliese didn't look up.

"It's okay," she said. Then she turned her pale blue eyes on him, and they weren't the eyes of an angelfish anymore, but maybe of a barracuda in training. Filled with warning. "For now, anyway," she added.

♦

So things returned to normal, more or less. Bellamy got his act together. It wasn't easy with all those eyes watching him for the slightest screw-up. He never complained. He was a pretty good teacher. Even Garnet had to admit it. Outside the classroom he kept to himself, and that was just fine. Somebody else took over the math team.

Brody waited after class for Garnet and Annaliese and always had a question for them about how their day had been. Annaliese learned to laugh without being asked.

Ick had brought them even closer together, and Annaliese, for one, was not about to forget it. The white spot on her right earlobe never seemed to fade away. For a good long time it was the only makeup she wore.

THE BERMUDA TRIANGLE

Jim wrapped himself around the top of the tree like a flag around a pole. The September sky swayed in a slow circle above him, the tree in a slow circle under him. He got his breath, pushed his nerves down hard into the steel trap of his stomach, closed the lid on his fear. Then he waited a moment, breathing deeply, pumping himself up.

There was a wind up here. And a view. Locking his legs tightly around the tree trunk, Jim dared to let go with one hand. He was a sailor riding the crow's nest of a schooner. And there — the road past the farm — that was the sea. There was a good chop on it, for the pavement was cracked and heaving. It was a forgotten sea in a forgotten corner of the county.

Billy Bones was out there on that choppy sea in his '55 De Soto sedan, a frigate of steel and chrome. It plied the broken road in great springy leaps, bellying out between the buckles, the chassis scraping the road top. Billy headed up towards the highway. Then he drove back down a few moments later, heading towards his farm.

Jim started his tree swaying in the direction he wanted it to go. He held on with one hand, riding the tree now, leaning, leaning. It was maybe three metres to the next tree, another cedar, a twin in size to his mount. His dad would have said it was three yards. Either way, it would be his biggest leap so far.

Concentrate, Jim told himself. But then Billy Bones drove by again, up to the highway and back down.

What was he up to? Was he picking up his mail at the lockbox one letter at a time? Was this what he did with his time? Was he as touched in the head as people said?

Jim turned his attention back to the task at hand. He gulped in fistfuls of air, swinging out and out, leaning, untangling his limbs from the tree until there wasn't much holding him. Then he was... leaping...falling...grabbing...holding on for dear life.

He pressed his body into the green embrace of the cedar, which swayed and dipped with the weight of him so near its crown. The fir tree poked him in the face, the gut, scraping his skin, cutting his hands. But it was okay; he'd made it. Tightly he held on. He glanced behind him. The other tree still swayed with the memory of his weight in its branches.

It had happened again. Just as he leaped — just when there was nothing left to hold on to — he had made that sound. It started in his throat, and then it was outside him. A voice. *His* voice. He had a voice again.

He tried to speak, just say his own name. Nothing. It was gone. He could scream. Why couldn't he talk?

Beyond the trees Billy Bones sailed his navy blue

and cream yellow trawler up to the highway and back. Up and back, as if he were on patrol. Then, as Jim got his breath back, Billy coasted to a stop just near Jim's driveway. He climbed out of his car and looked up towards Jim, swaying against the slowly circling September sky.

Billy Bones scratched his head, looked out at the road. Looked as if maybe he were lost.

Jim slithered down through the branches, lithe as a squirrel — a flying squirrel — and landed with a thump on the grass. Billy was coming towards him up the drive. Jim watched him carefully, his fists clenched. He was ready to intercept the old guy, turn him around, send him home if he was going to tell on him.

"I seen your boy, Mrs. Hawkins, flying from tree to tree. Thought you'd want to know."

Who'd believe him anyway? The old man was touched in the head.

Billy came right up to Jim. He pointed to the car. "Runned outa gasoline," he said. "Got any gasoline on you, have you?"

Jim shook his head.

Billy looked towards the barn. Jim followed his gaze. For a minute he imagined his father coming out of the barn, coming to see what was up. But he didn't have a father anymore. Maybe Billy didn't know that. It was hard to guess what Billy might know.

Billy stared back out at his car. His shoulders fell. "You seen the box they got out there?" he said, pointing vaguely towards the road. "They got one of those box things out there on the road, *our* road. You seen it?"

Jim shook his head.

"Sure," said Billy. "One of those jobs from the Dee-partment of Highway Robbery. Got a long snake of a cord running out from it across the road. No doubting what that's for..."

He was agitated. His limbs jerked. Jim just held his ground. Waiting.

"That's right," said Billy, as if Jim had spoken. "A counter, see. Every time a car crosses that rubber cord, the box thing totes it up. That way they can tell how much this road is travelled upon."

Getting nothing, no reaction, from Jim, Billy looked out at the De Soto, scratched his chin, wiped his nose on the sleeve of his grimy jacket. Jim looked out at the road, too. Relaxed a bit. Billy hadn't come to tell on him.

Billy laughed. It was kind of like a series of hiccups. He didn't sound as if he'd had much practice laughing.

"I'll show 'em!" he said lustily, shaking his fist at the road. "I'll show that Dee-partment of Highway Robbery just how much traffic goes up and down our road. Do you know how many cars drove this road today?"

Jim shifted his weight, said nothing.

"Well, I'll tell you: thirty-six." Billy's old skin glowed with satisfaction, made him look as if there were rust around his eyes, his scabby lips.

Jim hadn't seen any cars go by today. Not anyone but Billy.

Billy laughed. "The traffic was all *me*."

He must have thought Jim had given him a look because he cussed the boy suddenly. "You'll laugh out the other side of your face when they put down a spanking new asphalt pavement, boy. See what I'm getting at?"

Jim waited. This was what you did. Eventually people got the message that you couldn't talk to them and backed off. People who weren't touched in the head, that is.

The glow seeped away from Billy Bones' face. Now his skin looked like weathered barn board. But he stuck out his chin. "This week a thousand damned cars'll drive up our side road, Jim Hawkins. You see it? See the beauty of it? I'm sending a message. I'm getting us a road. A *real* road."

Then Billy's face cracked open to reveal a mouthful of teeth so crooked no dee-partment could have set them straight. He tapped the side of his head to show where he kept the machinery that had come up with this brainy idea. "Crazy like a fox," he said.

Jim stood as still as a tree. Waiting. Watching.

"Oh, I've heard all about you, Jim Hawkins. You ain't so dumb as you let on, are you, boy?" Billy turned and looked with confident expectation around the yard. There was no one. His expression crumpled. He looked back at Jim. "I'm sorry 'bout your dad," he said.

♦

They were neighbours, but until that September day Jim had never met Billy or even seen him up close. He was to see him three times that fall — three startling times — then never again.

The second time was on a dark late afternoon in October with the sun, too early, making its excuses on the horizon. Jim was out with a stick in the cornfield defeating an army of stubble that rose in sorry ranks around him. There was a dog with him. Not his dog — he had no pet — but a dog that seemed to materialize out of thin air if you took to running through a field with a stick in your hand. Maybe it was the cornfield's own dog, for its hide was the colour of corn husks.

Jim was looking for more trees to conquer. Trees close enough together in size and distance that he might leap from one to the other, but far enough apart to make it a challenge. It was only when he was airborne that he could speak. Not words, maybe, but sound. And that was something. If he could find two perfect trees far enough apart, maybe he could get out a whole sentence. The sentence would be "Where are you, Dad?"

He had stopped speaking when his father went missing. When they found the empty car at the end of a trail deep in the woods. So Jim waited. He waited through the police investigation, through the memorial service, through his mother trying to explain what could not be explained. How in this world could a person just go missing? There didn't seem to be anything left to say.

The cornfield dog took to barking. Caught up in the excitement, that's what Jim thought till he realized that the dog was standing square now, barking at some real enemy. Jim swung around, and there, coming across the rugged ground, was Billy Bones, waving something in his hand. Jim grabbed hold of the end of his long stick, held it up like a pikestaff. Stood, like the dog, square to the invader.

It was not a weapon old Billy was waving. It was

paper. Beyond him was the overgrown windbreak that surrounded Billy's shack, and for a moment Jim wondered if he had trespassed on the old man's fields. But the paper wasn't like that, a deed, or whatever, though he waved it like one. He waved it like an accusation at Jim.

"Can you believe it?" he shouted when his wobbly legs had carried him close enough to be heard over the dog's infernal barking. "Can you believe they'd do such a thing?"

Jim wondered if it was the Dee-partment of Highway Robbery again. They had not fixed the road, though Billy had kept up his lonely petition for a week or more. As if his '55 De Soto were a pen, he had written, if not a thousand, at least a few hundred signatures on that road. Jim had even watched him from his bedroom window late one night, travelling up and down, tripping that wire, piling up the numbers.

Now Billy came closer. He was worked up. There was spit hanging out one side of his mouth. Then suddenly he seemed to notice the stick in Jim's hands, and his eyes swam with confusion. He held the paper up to his chest. Jim lowered the stick. The dog stopped barking, sat down. Billy edged closer.

"Can you read, Jim Hawkins? Can you?"

Jim did his statue routine. There was nothing in his eyes but the lowering October sky. Billy dared to step over the last hill of cornstalk rubble that separated them until they were face-to-face. He showed Jim the piece of paper. It was a clipping from a newspaper. There was a drawing at the top — a poor, childish drawing of a poor, mean building. A castle. Above it in handwritten letters it said, "Fairyland."

"They're selling it," said Billy, grabbing the clipping back to look at it again. "They're selling Fairyland. There's going to be an auction. Says right here. Can you read, Jim Hawkins?"

Jim didn't say.

"I'll read it to you," said Billy.

Fairyland, established in 1912, will be sold by public auction on Nov. 15, at 2:00 P.M. Open house, Nov. 14. 104 acres, has 1.3 km frontage, Trans-Canada Highway. Presently 20 acres are developed into an amusement park and consist of a giant playground, 18 hole miniature golf, boating pond, fairy-tale forest, 50-seat miniature train, canteen, souvenir shop, etc., etc.

Billy read the whole thing out loud, looking up furtively from time to time as if he thought Jim might just decide to hit him with his stick. Jim stood stock-still, listening. His father used to read to him. But nobody had read to him in a long while.

When Billy finished, Jimmy took the advertisement from him and looked it over. It was yellowed.

Fairyland, it turned out, was a long way away. Prince Edward Island. The owner wished to retire, the clipping said. And the date of the auction was November 15, 1983. The auction had already happened more than a dozen years ago. Jim handed the clipping back to Billy.

Billy looked it over again, shaking his head. His

lips were closed tight. One of his teeth poked out the side. He looked away wistfully, checked the clipping one more time. Then he folded it and stuffed it into the chest pocket of his overalls.

The dog suddenly took off. Maybe someone had whistled with a secret dog whistle. Or maybe it had sensed another boy with a stick in some other field.

"Buried a treasure there," said Billy Bones, patting his chest pocket. "In a tin biscuit box, outside the roller-coaster ride."

He looked sideways at Jim, then flinched as if the boy might yell at him for being an idiot.

"I was eleven, about. Your age. We was camping down the road a bit. I snuck out from the tent one night, snuck myself into Fairyland and buried my treasure. In a biscuit tin. Right outside the roller-coaster ride."

Jim hugged his stick to him, leaned on it. Listened. Far away he heard the cornfield dog barking.

"I drawed a map," said Billy Bones, licking his cracked lips. His eyes were flitting as if in a dream. "I was gonna trick my kid brother. We was gonna *find* that map somewhere. Maybe on the beach near where we was camped. 'Lookit, Johnnie. Lookit here.' And there'd be the map wrapped up in a old piece of cloth, a old piece of oilskin. 'It's a treasure map. Must be a hundred years old, Johnnie.'"

Billy laughed his dry-bones laugh. "We'd have ourselves a high old time," he said. "Tracking down that treasure. Tracking it right into Fairyland."

Jim opened his mouth then. No words came out, but Billy seemed to sense he was asking him something.

"What was in it, Jim? Is that what you want to know?"

Billy sniffed. Scratched. He made as if to fish the clipping out of his pocket again, as if maybe there'd be a clue there. "I don't recall, exactly. Not all of it. I know I packed that biscuit tin tight, though." He dug and dug in his memory. Found something. "There was a skull of some small bird. I put a penny in both its eyeholes. I remember that."

He paused, shivered a bit. "I remember that," he said again, as if each penny required a separate memory. Then he shook his head. Jim could almost see Billy scrabbling with his old fingers at the top of that buried treasure box. Scratching away the tamped-down earth. Wanting to see inside it again, so far away. Then Billy's arms fell to his sides in defeat.

"I buried the map on the beach," he said. "I had it all set up. We'd find the map and then go after the treasure. And you know what, Jim? My dad packed us up the very next morning, and we left. No one told me why. We left, and we never come back."

He stared at Jim. Cricked his neck a bit as if trying to peer inside Jim's turbulent brown eyes, clear into his head to see what was cooking there. Then he straightened up. Looked around, wrapped his arms about himself as if he'd just realized that it was late in October and too cold to be standing in the middle of a field talking with a silent boy.

"We had come there every summer, Jim. Every danged summer. Now it's gone."

Billy bit on his lip. Then he kicked the ground with his scraped old boot. He hardly made an impression on the dried mud. The frost was already in the ground.

"Fathers do mysterious things," he said.

Then, as abruptly as he had arrived, he turned and marched back towards his place.

♦

It snowed late in November, winter knocking on the door. But the seasons weren't about to stop Jim from his quest. He had found himself two perfect trees right on the property line. He looked up, shielding his eyes from the fat, lazy snowflakes. The tops of the trees were two grown men apart. A leap of two grown men. You could fit a whole long sentence into such a jump.

Jim started to climb. He climbed swiftly.

"Look at me, Dad," he said inside his head. "Look at how far I can go." As he clambered from branch to branch, he recalled a summer day when he was little, climbing the apple tree in the yard. His father had stopped fixing the tractor to come and watch. "You scamp," his father said, wiping his greasy hands on a rag. "We should have called you Sir Edmund Hillary."

"Look how high," said young Jimmy. "Look, Dad." He turned to make sure his father was watching. And in that moment of distraction his foot slipped and his hand missed its hold and he fell. But his father caught him.

Jim stopped in his climb, hugged the pine tree tight. With his eyes clapped shut he could smell the grease on his father's hands holding him tight and safe.

The memory passed. He looked down. Directly

below, far below, was a split rail fence and all along its length thornbushes and piles of stones that his father and his father before that and who knows how many fathers had deposited there, for stones were the biggest crop in this part of the world.

Fence, thornbush and stone. And nobody to catch him.

He reached the top. He swung the tree angrily, silently swearing at it like a rider on a stubborn animal.

"Take me away from here!" he wanted to say. "Take me away!"

How could there be no clues at all? How could his father just disappear? In mystery books, things were always found: the treasure, the missing person. So if this wasn't a mystery, what was it? Nothing. And what could you say about nothing?

Farther and farther he bent that pine until it fairly whipped him through the snowy air. His eyes squinted through the snowflakes at his treetop target. One, two, three —

He would have leaped for sure if something hadn't caught his eye and made him think a thought outside his anger. Distracted him. Brought him up short.

It was two things, really.

He saw his own house across the field. He saw smoke coming from the chimney. Nothing strange about that. He'd chopped the wood himself. Lighting the morning fire was now his work. But then, as he swayed with greater and greater force, bending the tree to his wild purpose, his eyes took in another chimney, the chimney of Billy Bones' place. He could see it just over the windbreak.

There was no smoke coming out of Billy's chimney.

He stopped. It was like waking up from a nightmare. Suddenly he was frightened and clung to the tree for dear life.

He made his way down and across the cornfield — a treachery of ice — and through the windbreak the way he had seen Billy go. He came out in Billy's yard.

The DeSoto was in a shed, covered over with a tarp as if it were Billy's secret destroyer, only called into action to take on the forces of the dee-partments of the world.

The door to the shack where Billy lived was open a bit. Snow filmed the threshold. Jim stepped inside. He had noticed an outhouse, but one whiff inside Billy's shack led him to believe it had been a long time since the old man had made his way out to it. Breathing through his mouth, Jim looked around. The ceiling was low, the windows gummy with grime. In the dimness and the clutter of dilapidated furniture, Jim saw lawn ornaments everywhere. There was a painted gnome standing in the sink, a black boy fishing amid the dirty dishes on the kitchen table. His line hung down to a floor so littered with crumbs that the only thing the black boy was likely to catch was a mouse.

A doe and a fawn leaned against a wall below a coatrack. Billy's greasy plaid jacket had fallen from a hook and hung over the fawn's head, blindfolding it.

Beyond the blinded fawn a door stood slightly

open. Jim heard a dry cough. He looked inside. Billy Bones lay in his bed, a comforter up around his ears. His chin was on his chest; his eyes flickered open. He saw Jim, peered at him.

"The wife left," he said. Though his voice was ghostlike, he spoke with such urgency that Jim turned as if he might still catch sight of her leaving. One look at the decrepitude of the front room, however, was enough to tell him that Billy's wife must have left a long time ago. He'd never heard of any wife.

"Took everything," Billy said. "Everything."

Jim stepped into the bedroom. He looked around. He reached out to touch the peeling wallpaper. The wall was glazed with frost.

Billy's chin had fallen to his chest again. Jim turned on his heels and went out of the shack. Beside the porch he found some wood and an axe. He split some wood to kindling, gathered an armful and set about making a fire in the woodstove. There were piles of aging newspapers handy for tinder. Maybe it was in lighting a fire that Billy had happened upon the news of the sale of Fairyland. Jim didn't stop to read the pages now. Soon he had a good fire going. He checked the chimney for leaking smoke.

He ventured back into the bedroom, over to Billy's bedside. Billy woke up again, though his eyes did not fully open. He licked his lips. Jim went to the kitchen to get him a glass of water. He had to pump the water up. It splashed on the gnome in the sink, brightening to blue a patch of his filthy jersey. Jim poured a cup of the water on the gnome's leg.

The dust was washed away to reveal pants as red as the deepest fire. Jim wanted suddenly to wash that gnome and polish it clean. But a cough from the bedroom reminded him why he was there, what he was doing.

Billy had propped himself up in his bed. He reached for the water greedily but sipped at it timidly, as if his thirst were a great deal larger than his capacity to swallow. He cleared his throat, spit on the floor. It was still chilly. Jim wondered if the heat from the stove would ever reach this far.

"Left. Just like that," said Billy. He sniffed. "Can you believe it?" His head fell back on the pillow as heavily as if it were filled with plaster. Jim put the glass down on the bedside table. Billy looked longingly at a bookshelf across the room. He slid his arm out from under the covers and pointed with a gnarled finger towards something. Jim followed his gaze and walked over to the bookshelf. He held up one thing after another: an alarm clock, a ship in a bottle, a jar of small change, a book lying open. None of these things was what Billy wanted.

"The box," he said.

On his haunches, Jim explored the shelves. A biscuit tin. He remembered Billy's buried treasure and opened it. There was no bird's skull with pennies in its eyes. There were only stamps.

"Bring it here, Jim."

Jim carried the tin over to Billy, who propped himself up again so he could finger through the contents.

"I used to collect stamps," he muttered. "Collect them proper, in books. There was a stamp club in town, met once a month in the museum there."

He held up a stamp to the pale light coming from his window. It was the face of a man — a president or prime minister. He put it back in the box.

"She took the whole danged thing," said Billy. "The whole collection. Books and books."

He took a few shallow breaths. Held up another stamp. It was of a black king in tribal robes.

"Sold 'em, I guess. Worth something. You can believe that."

He held up a third stamp, larger than the rest. A triangular stamp, brightly coloured.

"Ahhh," said Billy, smiling, "but she didn't get it all."

It was a pirate with flaming red hair. Jim reached out to have a look at it. The pirate had a cutlass raised, a rich gold damask waistcoat and breeches, a gold chain around his neck.

"It's all I got left," said Billy.

Jim looked in the tin, fingered through the stamps. There were other triangular stamps. They were all pirates, six of them. The stamps were from Bermuda.

"They're beauties, eh?" said Billy. Jim nodded. There was Captain William Kidd, Henry Morgan, Edward Teach, known as Blackbeard, Mary Read, Bartholomew Roberts and Jean Lafitte. Each stamp was a different denomination. Blackbeard's was two dollars.

Billy took the Blackbeard stamp from Jim. He looked at it proudly. "Two Bermuda dollars, Jim. Little red-coloured bills, half the size of ours — saw one once." He sniffed. "You could send a parcel anywhere with a stamp like that on it."

Billy handed Jim the stamp. Edward Teach had three pistols in his belt and a glint in his lunatic eyes. His beard was plaited in four braids, laced with gold ribbon.

"When they brung that series out, they called 'em the Bermuda triangles."

Billy Bones took to coughing then. He coughed so much that Jim put the box of stamps down on the bedspread in case he was needed, though he could think of nothing to do to help. When the bout was over, Billy lay back on his pillow, exhausted.

Billy looked at him. Looked hard. "What happened to your voice, boy? You lose it somewhere?"

Jim picked up the box of stamps, looked at the Bermuda triangles one by one. Put the top back on the tin. Put the tin back on the shelf where he had found it.

He shuddered, cleared his throat. Opened his mouth, closed it, opened it. He thought of words, gave shape to them with the muscles of his face, his tongue. He took a deep breath. But in the silence just before speech, he heard Billy snore. He shut his mouth.

Jim stoked the fire, piled it high with the driest wood he could find, then turned the damper way down, the better to keep it burning. He opened the icebox to see if there was any food he could leave for Billy beside his bed, but the stench was horrible. He would come back with something from home. Load the fire up again.

He did that for two days, checking on the old man each time. Feeding him a bit of soup. A thermos cup of tea. He discovered other biscuit tins with other treasures in them: buttons, marbles, the wings of butterflies.

The third day he came up the buckled road, he saw an ambulance at Billy's house. He watched it pull away in a swirl of snow. He stopped in his tracks, wrapping his arms around the pot of soup he'd brought. When the ambulance was out of sight, he went on to Billy Bones' shack. The man was gone. The tin of stamps was gone as well.

He sat at the kitchen table beside the black boy fishing and drank some of the soup. Many-bean soup. One of Mom's specialties. It was good.

◆

Billy Bones died.

"I feel like it's my fault," Jim wrote on the kitchen pad.

His mother shook her head. "You did all you could. As soon as you told me about his condition, I called the district health nurse. They were checking in on him, too, honey."

Jim had been going to talk to Billy. He had felt the words almost come out. Safer to try it on someone not expecting too much, someone touched in the head. Someone who seemed always to be losing things himself.

◆

It was a week after Billy died that a strange thing happened. A parcel arrived for Jim Hawkins, wrapped in brown paper and string. The stamp on it was the two-dollar Bermuda Blackbeard. It had even been cancelled at the post office, as if the parcel had really come from Bermuda. There was no return address.

When Mrs. Hawkins handed Jim the package, there was something more than curiosity — there was concern in her eyes. She looked at him as if there were a world of things she didn't know about him, her own son.

Inside the package was the tin box of stamps, including the five remaining pirates. Jim carefully removed Blackbeard from the wrapping paper. He lined the pirates up on his mother's shining table top.

"What is all this then, Jim?" said his mother, stopping to look over his shoulder. Jim gathered his strength together. He opened his mouth, closed it, opened it again. Once again he thought of words, gave shape to them with the muscles of his face, his tongue. He took a deep breath. He leaned out towards the words, reaching, grabbing, squeezing them out of himself into the muffin-smelling air of his mother's kitchen.

"I guess it's a gift," he said.

THE ANNE REHEARSALS

It is Anne of Green Gables' birthday, and we are celebrating: Deirdre, Koko and me. We call ourselves the Rillas. The Rillas are having tea using the company china. On Anne's birthday we Rillas always try to do things just right.

Deirdre has an Anne of Green Gables cookbook. I wanted to make Rebecca Dew's angel cake, but Mom said it took too many eggs. In the end we made liniment cake, the one Anne made for the minister's wife. Except, of course, we didn't use anodyne liniment, as Anne did. We used vanilla extract, which was what Anne intended to use — but you probably know that if you know anything about Anne.

We had to quadruple the liniment cake recipe because we wanted to make a cake in the shape of Prince Edward Island. It was my idea. And we pulled it off, pretty much. Malpeque Bay didn't work out so well, and my brother, Sterling, ate Cape Bear before it was even iced, but otherwise it's pretty good. And the icing? Green — what else?

Prince Edward Island may be very small, but it makes for a very big cake. We pooled our resources and bought 121 candles. We're still trying to light them. We've gone through half a box of matches and only half the island is lit up. By the time we get to Tignish, the candles at East Point will have melted down to nothing.

"Why don't you use a flamethrower?" says Sterling.

We banish Sterling to the basement and lock the door.

I stamp my foot in a very Anneish manner. "Things seem to be going to the demnition bow-wows!"

Deirdre and Koko laugh nervously. It's hard to laugh when you're holding a lighted match. The demnition bowwows is something Maud Montgomery used to say. She wrote the Anne books. It's one of our favourite sayings.

"One, two, three!"

Each of us strikes another match simultaneously and starts lighting.

"Ow!" That's Deirdre. It's the third time she's burned herself. "Next time let's get those number candles," she says.

"We'll probably still be lighting this cake by then," says Koko with despair.

We keep lighting, as the candles on the Atlantic coast of the cake waver and flicker.

"Ow!"

Poor Deirdre. I think it's because she's left-handed that she's so clumsy. She drew the portrait of Anne of Green Gables that graces the front of our Anne scrapbook. It is very talented. Deirdre will be a great artist. But if you look up close, the lines on the picture are all smudged a bit, on account of Deirdre dragging her hand across the page. It must be awful to be left-handed. But here's the thing: many artists are.

There. It's done.

"Eheu!" shouts Koko.

"Eheu!" shout Deirdre and I, blowing out our matches.

It's another thing Maud used to say. We have no idea how it's supposed to be pronounced, so we say it kind of like a samurai sneezing. "Eee-*huww*!"

"The lights!" I cry.

Koko turns off the overhead lights. It's only four-thirty but it's already dark outside. That's what you get if your birthday is on November 30.

"Mom!"

Mom is in her office on the phone. Great.

"Quick, Mom. Before the candles go out."

I hear Mom's hurry-up voice. She's supposed to take pictures. Her voice isn't hurrying up enough. The whole green island seems to be wavering. I grab her camera and try to remember all the stuff about f-stops. It's a real camera; Mom's a real photographer. The camera doesn't aim by itself or do anything for you. She has shown me how it works, but under pressure I've gone all stupid. I snap off a picture. The flash goes off.

"That's no good," says Deirdre. "With the flash we won't be able to see the candles."

"Mom!"

"Coming, coming," she says. But it seems like an hour before she appears.

"It was only ten seconds," she says as she takes the camera from my hands and expertly screws it onto her tripod. "I was watching my watch," she adds.

"What a good thing to do with a watch," I say a little peevishly, because she's such an expert.

"Hey, let me out!" says Sterling. He's trying to open the door from the basement.

"Carmen."

"He ate Cape Bear."

Mom is looking through the viewfinder. "Carmen, let your brother out of the basement. Now."

Deirdre and Koko are laughing, but I'm watching Prince Edward Island burn to the ground.

"Carmen!"

"Okay, okay!"

I let Sterling in and then race back to join Deirdre and Koko behind the cake. We put our arms around one another and bend low so that our faces will glow in the candlelight. We smile, though I'm sure my smile will look horrible. I meant to take off my retainer. Anne didn't wear braces. They are completely unpoetical.

Mom pulls through.

Click, click, click, click, click.

Then one with Sterling. Mom insists. He hams it up, as usual. He raises his hands over the cake like a monster about to scarf down the whole thing. Deirdre and Koko laugh, but I don't. He's stealing the show.

"'You have inclinations, child, which run counter to our compulsion!'" I tell him. Maud Montgomery again. Sterling pays no attention.

"Cut it out, Sterl," says Deirdre.

To my surprise, he does.

Click.

"That's a wrap," says Mom.

"Oh, just one more, Mom," I say. "When we blow it out."

"Hey," says Sterling, "can I help?"

He's already filling his cheeks with air when I drag him off. We're not interested in his eight-year-old air. We have other ideas.

"Anne's going to blow out the candles herself," I tell him.

Sterling actually looks surprised.

On cue, Deirdre and Koko go to the French doors. They swoosh the doors open. A cold November wind sweeps into the dining room, and all of Anne's 121 candles bend before it.

Click.

Happy birthday, Anne. I hope you made a wish.

◆

We make faces and gagging noises as we eat the cake, as if it really did have anodyne liniment in it. Sterling just eats. He doesn't care one bit about Anne of Green Gables.

"It isn't even her birthday," he says.

I hold up my fork ready to stab him.

"Carmen."

I put down my fork. What I can't figure out is how Sterling knows that it isn't really Anne's birthday. November 30 is Maud Montgomery's birthday. We know that, but how does he?

Koko stops eating with a forkful of cake raised halfway to her lips. "I heard something terrible the other day," she says. "P.E.I. is moving."

We all stop eating.

"Where to?" says Deirdre. "The States?"

She looks so shocked we all laugh.

Then Koko explains. The eastern part of the island is wearing away from the constant battering of the Atlantic Ocean. Prince Edward Island is pretty much all sand, after all.

"So it's getting smaller," I say. "That's not like moving."

Koko puts down her fork. "But that's the weird thing. You see, the sand that's washed away is silting up on the western end of the island, making it longer. So it's kind of like it's moving."

"Hey," says Sterling, "you guys should be happy."

"He's right," says Deirdre, who somehow understands Sterling. "It's moving closer to us."

I imagine Prince Edward Island worming its way down the St. Lawrence River. I imagine waking up one morning and looking out my window, and there it is, bumping up lightly against our front porch. I imagine stepping from our front step onto a green meadow complete with a red soil pathway leading to a perfect one-room schoolhouse.

"Could this really be true?"

Mom watches her watch again. "Should be here in a couple of million years."

Sterling sits back. He's just finished eating most of the southwest shore. "It's just following Lucy Montgomery," he says.

The room grows silent. We Rillas turn on him with daggers in our eyes. Sterling looks frightened.

"I just meant she moved to Ontario, too. Didn't she? Remember, we saw her place in Toronto and — hey, what is this?"

"You have committed the cardinal sin," says Deirdre.

"You'd better say your prayers," says Koko.

I grab Sterling by the collar, pull his face up close, and give him the evil eye. He looks really good and scared.

"Don't ever...*ever*...call her Lucy. She hated the name. And so do we. Understand?"

Sterling nodded.

"Apologize," I say.

Sterling looks to Mom for help. She raises her hands as if helpless to save him. I tighten my grip.

"Okay, okay!" he says. "I'm sorry."

"Don't apologize to me," I say. "Apologize to Maud."

Sterling rolls his eyes, but he does it. He gets up and opens the door and shouts into the November darkness, "Sorry, *Maud*."

Deirdre rewards him with another slice of cake, but he's not hungry anymore and leaves the room. He sticks his tongue out at me. He doesn't realize that he got off easy!

◆

I'm lying in bed thinking about Maud. It's still her birthday, and I'm wondering how a great author celebrates her birthday. Alas, her husband, Ewan, was not a kindred spirit. He was a minister. He was also a bit of a basket case. Poor Maud. But whatever her personal life was like, she had her books. I've read them all.

I shift in my bed so I can see the framed photograph Mom took of me when we went to Green Gables. I'm standing in the Haunted Woods. I can't really see the picture, but I know what's there. And I think of something a biographer wrote about Maud, how she had this "tormenting need to purge her soul of its ecstasy in verbal expression." I know what that's all about. I love writing. I can taste words. Some taste like copper, and some like licorice, and some taste like liniment cake. The best words taste like the nectar in clover.

"Oh, Maud," I whisper, "help me to become a writer. I promise that all my stories, like yours, will end happily."

♦

I was the one who named us the Rillas: Deirdre, Koko and me. *Rilla of Ingleside* is about Anne Shirley's daughter. Maud set the book during the war years — World War I. Maud wanted it to be a tribute to the girlhood of Canada. Since we are the girlhood of Canada, the Rillas is a perfect name for us. Sterling calls us the gorillas. Sterling is beyond endurance.

Deirdre and I discovered Anne together. She's read all the books, too. Not just the Anne books, either, but the Emily series and the Sarah Stanley stories.

Koko's mother grew up in Japan. Anne Shirley was her hero. In fact, she met Koko's father in Charlottetown when she went as a tourist to see Green Gables. She wore a red wig and painted freckles on her beautiful Japanese face. So did everybody on the tour. All those Japanese Annes. She laughs about it now. She says, "If Kurt fell in love with me looking like that, he must *really* love me."

I think about that. And I think about Prince Edward Island moving west, and for some reason that all gets mixed up with how smart Sterling is getting when he's not even nine yet. Nothing stays the same.

◆

Mom is fuming. It's the pictures she took of our Anne party. I wonder if they've come out underexposed or out of focus. It's hard to imagine Mom making such a mistake. She can hardly even speak, she's so cross. She thrusts the photos at me, but out of nowhere Sterling swoops by, grabbing the package out of my hands.

"Cool!" he says.

I lift my school binder over my head, prepared to brain him. Mom stops me. "Sterling," she says. Flinging the package towards me, he dashes out of the room. I miss the package. I say something I am not permitted to say, but Mom is too angry herself to notice. I bend down to pick up the photographs, staring in disbelief.

There is a picture of a kid sitting on a camel, a fat, balding man with a little girl in his arms pointing at a sleeping tiger, a monkey swinging blurredly in a cage.

These aren't our pictures. They aren't even people we know.

"Mom?"

She's already on the phone to the photo place. "Don't tell me there can't be a mistake," she is saying. "You think I don't know my own children?"

There are no pictures of the Rillas, no pictures of our fabulous cake.

"What do you mean, you'll give me a free roll of film?"

With a gasp I think of our Anne scrapbook. I've already composed the captions for the pictures.

"Yes, I want to talk to the manager. Face-to-face. I'll be right down."

Mom hangs up and grabs the photos from me. Her eyes are flashing. She loves a good squabble. My own eyes are stinging. I am suddenly overcome with dread. A premonition. This is just the first taste. Something awful is going to happen.

◆

My premonition is right.

It doesn't seem bad at first. In fact, it seems miraculous. The very next day Mrs. Ginger, the music teacher, announces that the school is going to put on *Anne of Green Gables* as the end-of-the-year musical.

Koko breaks the news to us. She's absolutely breathless. Mrs. Ginger wants her to try out for the role of Anne. Koko has a beautiful singing voice, and I imagine her right away in a red wig and painted-on freckles just like her mother. "It was fated to happen, Kokey."

"Auditions aren't until January," says Koko. As soon as she says that, the delicious feeling starts to turn sour.

Auditions.

It doesn't bear thinking about. My mother says I can't carry a tune in a bag, and she's perfectly right. I'm just not musical. I can't play an instrument, either. The word *audition* tastes like dust on my tongue.

"There's some parts in the play where you don't really have to sing," says Deirdre, who can see the disappointment, the shame, written all over my face. She looks squeamish when she says it.

"Oh, thanks," I say very peevishly. "Luckily I'm a fabulous actress." And I storm away. Because of course I can't act my way out of a paper bag, either.

A week later Mr. Brunner, the art teacher, asks Deirdre to design and paint the backdrop. She asks me if I want to help. "Right," I said. "You can use me for a paintbrush. Painting is just one more talent I can't carry in that demnition bowwow paper bag!"

◆

The Christmas holiday comes. Koko always goes away to celebrate New Year's with her aunt and uncle in Vancouver. This year Deirdre goes away, too. To Phoenix. I'm almost glad. At least I won't have to listen to any more stuff about the big show. Koko is a shoo-in for the part of Anne. Everybody says so. But the nauseating thing is, she'd be happy just singing in the chorus. Oh, I hate myself for thinking like this. Koko is my very best friend, but right now her niceness is too much to bear.

◆

Sterling's birthday is on December 23. It's a horrible time for a birthday. Mom is always super busy at Christmas, doing family portraits and things. So I'm the one who has to be in charge of dear Sterling's birthday. This year he wants a theme party, a pirate party.

He is so unpoetical.

"Why me?" I plead with Mom. She gives me her

I-have-three-seconds-of-patience-left look. I stomp out of her studio.

That night I pray to Maud for guidance. That's when I recall that she used to direct plays at her husband's church. I imagine I'm Maud and that it is my duty to do a splendid job for the little people of the congregation.

It turns out to be sort of fun, really. It's nice to see all these little nine-year-old guys dressed as pirates when everywhere you look there's nothing but elves and jolly snowmen and enough Santas to give a reindeer a heart attack.

I throw myself into the party. What else is there to do when your best friends have deserted you? I cut up green bristol board to make palm leaves, which I hang decoratively around the living room. Deirdre would have made them better, but they don't look too bad. In fact, with a sandy-coloured blanket thrown over the couch and a stuffed parrot hanging from the bookshelf, by the time I'm finished, the living room looks like a desert island. There's even a huge conch shell we brought back from Florida. I arrange chocolate gold coins spilling out of it onto the aquamarine carpet. Very piratical.

Then the kids come. I give them all makeup scars and skull-and-crossbone tattoos. And there are games, too: pin the pegleg on Pete. The night before, I get Sterling to draw the pirate life size on a roll of newsprint, using me as an outline. We colour it in together. Very scary. Of course most of Sterling's friends actually try to pin the pegleg up Pete's nose, or worse!

I am a hit. Me, Carmen, a hit with a dozen fifth

graders. They listen to me; they do what I say, even Sterling. It's miraculous. Anyway, it takes my mind off you know what.

Sterling's three best friends get to stay the night. I tell pirate stories. I scare their little nine-year-old brains out!

That night in bed I try to figure why I'm so good at telling stories and so hopeless onstage. It's not that I can't remember lines. Maybe, I think, I'm just horribly selfish and want to say only my own words.

Christmas comes and goes. I get invited to a sleigh ride and skating party where no one even cares about the end-of-the-year musical. Anne of Green what?

But finally it's back to school, where suddenly everyone is totally Anne-crazy. The school is full of Anne-oholics, and I don't think any of them have even read the book! There are about 600 kids at our school. Approximately 562 are trying out for the show. I get flu the week of auditions. Surprise.

Koko gets Anne. I'm really thrilled for her. Really.

◆

The Anne rehearsals start in March. Kids are soon humming all the time. The songs are infectious.

"Ice cream. Da da da da da da da da da, ice cream."

Teachers have to stop kids from humming in the classroom. Guys who usually play soccer at recess are standing around stamping their feet on the last dirty crust of snow as they try to memorize lines. And Koko is over the moon, though she tries not to show it when she's around me. That's because I blew up one day.

"Can't you guys talk about anything else? It's Anne this and Anne that all the livelong day."

When I think about it later, it's a pretty weird thing for me to be saying. Of all people.

Deirdre is doing a huge mural of rolling fields and cherry trees in blossom with the town of Avonlea nestled prettily in a fold of the hills. I sneak into the gym to see it. She has never worked so big, and the best part is, working on a mural, she doesn't drag her hand over the stuff she's just finished drawing.

But what's this? One of the trees is leaking. There's a huge blossom pink pool. It covers half a cow! What is going on?

I don't mention it next time I see Deirdre. She looks pretty glum, and I was the one, after all, who said no more talk about the play.

The worst part is walking home after school, alone. As I pass the gym, I hear them singing. "Ice cream. Da da da da da da da da da da, ice cream."

I have no idea how much it's getting to me. Then one day Koko offers me a book to read. "I really think you'll like it," she says.

"And I have all the time in the world these days," I say, without even thanking her. I pretend not to notice how hurt she is. And then I have to notice because she's crying.

I try to say I'm sorry, but she runs away.

Then it's Deirdre's turn. One morning before class I notice her eyes are all bleary. I ask her what's the matter, and she just shakes her head. She doesn't want to talk about it. Not to me, anyway.

"What am I, the worst person in the universe?" I say to myself. Because by now there is no one else around to talk to. It's me. I am an insufferable hag. This is the one thing I *can* carry around in a paper bag: my utter hagness!

♦

The first day of spring arrives. I poke my head out the window, and the feeling of springness almost makes me dizzy. Without stopping to think, I call Koko and Deirdre immediately. I try not to notice how cool they sound. We walk to school together.

"It's as if spring has poked her head around the veil of winter, then checked her watch, hardly able to believe she's been asleep so long. She'll probably fall back asleep for a bit yet, but you can just feel she'll be up for good sooner or later."

Deirdre smiles a kind of dreary smile. Koko hardly seems to hear me at all. I'm afraid my heart is going to break.

"Kokey?"

"I hate this show!" she says.

I was about to fall humbly on my knees and beg her to forgive me. "You what?"

"I hate this show," she says again, perfectly clearly.

I find myself thinking a hateful thought: I'm glad she hates the show.

"But you're the star," I say. "You...you're Anne."

"It's not Anne," she says. "It's World War III!"

I feel dizzy. "Isn't it going well?"

Koko shakes her head violently. "Everybody's running around. You can hardly hear yourself sing, let alone think. Mrs. Ginger is hopeless. Hopeless!"

"Eee-*huww*!"

That's me. I make a few comical samurai chops in the air, which makes Koko smile a little.

Then Deirdre explains about the pink pond. Some boys were running around and knocked over her can of pink paint.

"Why didn't you tell me?" I ask. They glance at each other, and it's not hard to guess what they're thinking. "Don't answer that," I add.

◆

What can I do? I'm not surprised that Mrs. Ginger is hopeless. She can barely handle a classful of kids. She's little, for one thing. Probably only weighs about ninety pounds soaking wet, as my mom would say. A lot of the grade eight boys tower over her. And she wears sweater sets. With poodles on them.

"You'd have to see it to believe it," says Koko.

"Yes," I answer. "I was just thinking the same thing."

◆

So here I am at the gym after school, standing at the back by the doors, hoping no one will notice me watching the Anne rehearsal. It's as bad as Koko and Deirdre said. There're about a hundred kids in the cast. Some are sprawled over the stands to the left and right of the stage. They're what Mrs. Ginger calls the Greek chorus, though everyone is calling it the geek chorus. There are more people here than lived in Avonlea, probably. And everybody's running around, playing tag, gossiping, drinking pop and burping. They're all over the place, ants at a picnic.

I try to concentrate on what's going on up

onstage, a scene with Anne, Marilla and Matthew. Mrs. Ginger is at the piano, trying to concentrate. It isn't going well. Koko keeps looking at her script, and that is crazy because she had it memorized by Valentine's Day.

Deirdre seems to have hired a couple of grade eight thugs to stand guard so that no one runs over her backdrop, but she looks up every minute or two with a panic-stricken expression on her face. She sees me and holds up her hands in dismay.

Suddenly Mrs. Ginger seems to wake up and take notice of what's going on around her. She claps her hands sharply.

"Children!" she shouts in her feeble voice. "Children." She bangs her fists down on the piano, but nobody seems to take much notice. For one thing, we hate being called children.

Then Hugo Bovington, who plays Gilbert, puts his fingers to his lips and whistles ear-shatteringly. Mrs. Ginger winces, but now they all stop what they're doing.

Mrs. Ginger shakes her head. "Children," she says, "*Anne of Green Gables* is one of the most noble treasures of our literary heritage. It is an immortal classic. What do you think Lucy Montgomery would think of what is going on here?"

I feel faint. I have to lean against the door frame. I look at Deirdre. There is a look of mortal terror on her face. Her paintbrush drips green drops on a red barn. Koko is looking my way with the same look of horror. *Mrs. Ginger has committed the cardinal sin.* And it's up to me, as head of the Rillas, to set her straight.

"Mrs. Ginger?"

She doesn't hear me. So I shout, as loud as Hugo's whistle.

"Carmen. What is it? A message from the office?"

A message from the office. Is that all she thinks I'm good for? I walk a few paces forward. I'm down on the gym floor, but everyone is looking at me. It's as if I were up on the stage, and I have suddenly a huge case of stage fright. I clear my throat.

"No, ma'am. I don't have a message from the office. Actually, I have a message from Maud Montgomery."

There is an immediate buzz in the crowd, shushed just as quickly by those who want to hear what I'm going to say next.

"From whom?"

"Maud Montgomery," I say. My voice has a kind of eerie, wavering quality to it. That's how Koko describes it later, eerie and wavery. But it's really just nerves, the feeling that I might throw up any second.

Mrs. Ginger looks a bit confused. "From Lucy Maud, you say?"

"Not *Lucy* Maud, Mrs. Ginger. Just Maud. She wants you to know, wants you *all* to know, she *hated* being called Lucy."

There is genuine, pindrop quiet. I cannot believe it. Then somebody starts to snicker. And somebody else. A moment later the whole gym erupts with laughter. People are pointing at me, shaking their heads, holding their bellies. The geek chorus is falling over the stands and rolling on the floor. I am the biggest geek of them all!

◆

I run all the way home and sink into the deepest chair and the deepest depression. I am embarrassed beyond belief. But I'm angry, too. If only I could have said something. Not about Maud hating her first name. Something about the musical. About caring! For a moment I had the whole cast's attention. I could have issued a warning about what happens to people who are scornful of Maud Montgomery or of Anne.

It comes to me now. *The infamous incident at Ingleside*. A student cast that is so disrespectful that Maud sends the ghost of her faithful cat, Daffy, to haunt its production, a production that never makes it to opening night because at the dress rehearsal the ringleader of the troublemakers trips over the phantom cat and falls head first off the stage, breaking his wretched neck!

I'm so wrapped up in these dark and vengeful thoughts that I don't notice Sterling sneaking up behind me. Suddenly it's raining raisins. I grab him, and before he can call for help, I have him in a killer hold. Soon I have reduced the wiry little beggar to a rag doll pleading for mercy. I let him go.

But he doesn't go right away. He sits on the floor, leaning against my chair, popping raisins into his mouth. "When you had me upside down like that, I thought you were going to do what Captain Redeye did to the spy."

"Captain who?"

"You know, the story you told at my birthday party. It was great!"

Sterling isn't in the habit of complimenting me,

but it does little to improve my mood.

"You know what?" he says. "You should write about the musical for the newspaper."

I snort. The rag that the student council puts out once a month is nothing more than notices from the principal, a list of sports scores and upcoming school events.

Sterling reads my mind. "I mean the real paper," he says. "The *Courier*."

The town newspaper. I'm stunned.

"You always talk about becoming a writer. Well, here's your chance," he says. "You know more about Anne probably than anyone in the world."

I can't believe what I'm hearing. Before I know what I'm doing, I'm hugging him. Hugging Sterling. *Eheu!*

But the surprises aren't over yet.

"Isn't that how Anne started her career?" he asks.

◆

Well, to make a longish story short, I do it. The very next day, urged on by Deirdre and Koko, I go to see the editor of the *Courier*, who is very nice and, as luck would have it, very busy, with municipal elections coming up and all. She wants a piece of seven hundred words, which sounds immense. I think I'll never be able to write seven hundred words. But once I get going, I'm amazed at how much pours out, and the hardest job, in the end, is trimming it down. Maud guides my hand.

I write a bit about her, a bit about Anne, and a bit about the musical. I put aside my dark and vengeful thoughts; this is serious, my first published piece. Instead I write about how hard everyone at the school is working to make our Anne the best end-of-year production ever. Talk about stretching the truth. But then I've always liked fiction the best.

The article comes out accompanying pictures of the kids rehearsing. I even have a byline. "Special to the *Courier*, Carmen Stewart."

My geeky performance in the gym is soon forgotten once the paper hits the stands. Mrs. Ginger is over the moon about the article. It's the effect the publicity has on the cast. Suddenly the play is real! The public, not just parents, are going to come and see it. See them! Suddenly everyone is paying a lot of attention. Mrs. Ginger grins at me conspiratorially. "I'm sure Maud would be very gratified," she says.

◆

The show is great. The program even has a quote from my article on the cover with my name under it.

Understandably Koko gets most of the attention. She deserves it. She is sensational. And we Rillas, we're back together, tighter than ever.

But there's one truly spooky thing that happens. This chubby, balding man comes up to Koko on the first night of the run. I feel as if I've seen him somewhere before, so I edge closer. He has an envelope in his hands. I think he's just going to ask Koko for her autograph, but instead he takes a photo from the envelope. "Is this you?" he says.

It's Koko all right. And Deirdre and me and our fabulous Prince Edward Island cake. He is the one who got our photographs! That's where I had seen him, in the zoo shots.

My mother arranges to get the zoo photos back to the man. It seems he read my article and saw Koko's picture.

How great it is to see our pictures. How beautifully my braces gleam in the candlelight. How handsome Sterling looks. For a kid.

Which is a good way to end this story, with everything coming out happily. Just the way Maud would have wanted it.

THE FALLEN ANGEL

It was a late snowfall. A big one that lasted all night. Heavy enough to keep kids home from school. Heavy enough to bring down an angel.

Rodney saw the angel on his way to choir practice Thursday evening. The roads had been ploughed by then, and with the music festival coming up he couldn't afford to miss a practice. He was head chorister; he was supposed to set a good example. But more than that, it was his last music festival as a boy soprano. His voice was threatening to break. He only hoped it would hold off.

It was not dark yet. The clocks had already been set forward. The days were spring-loaded, and it seemed strange for it to be choir practice and only just twilight.

A snow angel — the perfect outline of it, anyway — on the steep sloping roof of the barn. There were no footprints, as far as Rodney could tell. Weird.

It wasn't a big barn. Mother had had it moved from the back end of the property in case she decided to raise something. One week she thought she'd raise chickens; the next, sheep. Maybe they'd get a donkey. Professor Dad called it her hobby barn. Whatever. Mom wanted that barn nearby. So a local farmer had hoisted it on the back of a flatbed and hauled it over. Now it sat among the freshly snow-laden trees on a rise out front near the road. Nestled prettily, it looked like a Christmas card, especially with the angel on it. For the time being, the only use the barn saw was as the neighbourhood drop for used clothing and toys and worn appliances for the local school's big spring rummage sale.

Rodney Adams lived where the town met the country. There was woodland between his house and town, but Rodney had made paths through it. That night the paths were clogged again with snow, so Rodney strapped on his snowshoes. For twenty minutes he would become Knut Svensson, wilderness adventurer.

Several times on a journey like this he might be called upon to fight off plague-mad mobs or fire off a few rounds at wolves that had gotten too close. He always fired over their heads. What with the plague and all, he understood their hunger. He himself had not eaten in months, not since before he crossed the North Pole. But with the precious serum in his pack, carried clear from Norway, doctors in these troubled parts could begin the process of stemming the deadly disease. Knut's song would be sung by all the thankful nations of the world.

A twig cracked behind him. A lone wolf? Knut hurled himself onto a steep snowbank, rolled over twice and fired back down the path. He lay in deep snow, catching his breath. He was looking west. The sun was on the horizon, glinting through the woods, throwing the trees and undergrowth into sharp relief.

He saw something move. For real. A shadow

only, perhaps, but a shadow had to have something real to hang on to. Rodney threw aside his rifle, a crooked ironwood branch, and, a little bit shaken, headed east towards the church.

As he came out of the woods, he met up with Claire, who was on her way to choir as well. She waited while he took off his snowshoes. He was covered from head to foot with snow.

"Lots of plague victims tonight?" she asked.

"More than you could shake a stick at," he said.

"Those guys," said Claire. "They'll do anything to get hold of the serum, won't they?"

Rodney blushed. One very cold Thursday night in January he had emerged like this from the woods covered in snow, and he had dared tell Claire about Knut Svensson, wilderness adventurer. She didn't make fun of him. She had adventures of her own, she said. He still hoped one day she'd tell him about them.

Now he told her about the snow angel on the barn roof.

"A fallen angel," she said.

Rodney laughed, imagining an angel stumbling over his heavenly skirts and tumbling — thump — onto the barn.

"Don't laugh," said Claire. "Satan was the first fallen angel."

"Yeah," said Rodney, "but he fell a lot farther than my roof."

Claire nodded thoughtfully, and the streetlight danced in her hair. There was an Irish folk song about a girl with nut-brown hair. Rodney always thought of Claire when he heard that song.

They joked around and dropped into Woodside Nick's to get some Meloids.

Only a singer would suffer Meloids. They were strong throat lozenges shaped like little shiny brown pellets. They came in flat tins and tasted worse than anything, but to the choristers of St. Mike's they were a badge. You sucked on a Meloid for a bit and thought, I am a singer.

As Nick's door slammed behind them, it brought an avalanche off the roof down on their heads. Claire screamed with surprise.

"More angels," said Rodney. He whooped with laughter, and his voice cracked. Claire pretended not to notice, but they both knew what it meant. Last year he had come second in the solo category. This year he was going for gold. There wasn't anyone in the city who could beat him. That is, if he still had a voice.

They walked on in silence until they arrived at the church. They were just going through the back door that led to the downstairs rehearsal hall when they noticed a boy following them. He looked about ten. He had curly black hair that fell long to his shoulders and across his eyes. He wasn't very big, and he looked smaller still in an oversized buckskin jacket with a fringe.

"Hi," said Rodney. "Are you here for choir?"

The boy smiled a loopy smile. "I don't know. Am I?"

"It's up to you," said Rodney. "Try it out if you like."

Kids showed up now and then, thinking maybe they wanted to sing in the choir. They were usually a little shy.

The boy shrugged, stuck his hands deep in his pockets. He looked around to see if maybe there was something else he could do.

"If you say so," he said.

Rodney glanced at Claire. She screwed up her nose as if she thought the kid was rude.

"I'm Rod. This is Claire."

"Luc," said the new boy.

◆

The new boy sat beside Rodney and shared his music. This was also one of Rodney's duties as head chorister, to show new kids the ropes. Luc didn't sing at first; then, when he did, his voice was too loud and cut through the other voices. In a choir your voice wasn't supposed to stand out.

"Very nice, Luc," said Mr. Whithorne, the choirmaster. "But half of singing in a choir is listening, blending in."

"If you say so," said Luc.

Rodney caught Claire's eye across the aisle. She was glaring. "If you say so." She mouthed the words with distaste.

◆

It was dark when practice was over. Moonless. Rodney had a flashlight on a strap that he could wear on his head if he wanted to be Knut Svensson, but tonight he just held it in his hand. He didn't feel like pretending. His mind was elsewhere. Back at St. Mike's. At the end of practice Mr. Whithorne had asked Luc to stay. As Rodney had left the church, he had heard Luc singing scales for the choirmaster. Beautiful, clear, ringing scales.

It was an uneventful journey: no madmen, no

wolves, no twigs snapping. Arriving home, he breathed a sigh of relief. His troubles were over, he thought.

But Professor Dad was displeased. Displeased was a lot like angry, but with a British accent.

"Ah, Rodney," he said, "perhaps you can shed some light on a little mystery we seem to be having."

John and Midge were sitting in the living room in a formal kind of uncomfortable way that suggested they hadn't been able to shed any light on the mystery and they sure hoped somebody would soon so that they could get on with what little bit of the evening was left before lights out.

Rodney joined his brother and sister. Mother smiled from the chair where she was knitting. "How was choir?" she asked.

Rodney said it was fine, but he could sense his father's impatience to get on with the proceedings.

"What's up?" he asked.

His father held up a Granny Smith apple with one bite out of it. "Exhibit A," he said. "Know anything about this?"

"No, sir," said Rodney.

"Dad found it beside the driveway," said Midge.

"Oh," said Rodney.

"How about this?" said his father, presenting a cake platter empty of anything but crumbs.

Rodney said, "Looks like the poppy seed torte we had last night. What's left of it."

"Precisely!"

"It wasn't me," said Rodney.

"Of course not," said Professor Dad. With

noticeable exasperation he put the platter, Exhibit B, down on the coffee table. "And it wasn't John and it wasn't Elizabeth, either."

"Hector," said Mrs. Adams, resting her knitting on her lap. "It's only a cake."

"And an apple," said Professor Dad.

"And an apple," Mother agreed.

"*And* the rest of the butter-brickle ice cream," said Professor Dad. He glared at each of the three children individually. It seemed that the disappearance of the butter-brickle ice cream was the real source of this hubbub.

"Are we being accused of stealing food?" said Rodney.

Mrs. Adams looked at her husband, raised her eyebrow. "Well, Hector?"

He took a deep breath. The three children exchanged surreptitious glances. With any luck that deep breath would be the end of the courtroom drama. There would be some sort of summary, and things would return to normal.

"As you well know," said Hector, "we put a good meal on the table in this establishment. We do not scrimp, nor do we begrudge you your snacks. You are all growing children, heaven knows.

"But I draw the line at gluttony. And I especially draw the line at waste. I won't have it." Once again he held up Exhibit A.

John, who was to turn eight next week, spoke up. "Throwing away an apple with only one bite out of it is criminal," he said. He said it with enough conviction that Hector's faith in his children seemed restored. For the time being, at least.

♦

Nobody in the Adams family went to church except Rodney. He had wandered into St. Mike's almost by accident. A kid at school had mentioned the choir, and he had ended up on the back steps the next Sunday, just like Luc. It turned out St. Mike's was a very good choir, an award-winning choir, and Rodney was now, four years later, not only the head chorister but also the soloist. This year he was singing the solo from Mendelssohn's *Hear My Prayer*. It didn't get higher than a G, but some days that was just a bit too high.

"'O, for the wings of a dove,'" he sang to himself as he set out for church Sunday morning through the woods in the once-again spring sun and through the once-again spring muck. He wore rubber boots and was too busy singing to save anyone from the plague. Yet, as he sang, he found his mind wandering. It was Luc who claimed his attention. His high, clear voice. Not really a good choir voice, but definitely solo material. Would he be at choir that morning? Rodney hoped not. Sometimes one rehearsal was enough to convince a kid that he wasn't really cut out for choir.

But Luc was there all right. Rodney came into the changing room to find Mrs. Hartwell, the choirmistress, consoling one of the younger boys. Luc was wearing the boy's surplice and cassock.

He sat beside Rodney during the service. Luc didn't show off when they were singing. In fact, he hardly sang at all. "I'm listening," he said when Rodney gave him a stern look. "That's what Mr. Whithorne said to do."

During the sermon Rodney whispered to him. "You know about Evensong, don't you?"

Luc didn't answer.

"We have to sing again this evening at seven. Didn't you know about that?"

Sometimes new kids didn't know about singing twice on Sundays and quit in disgust as soon as they found out.

"We have to be here at six-thirty for a practice," whispered Rodney. "The music is really boring. Canon Archibald usually does an extra-long sermon. It's really a drag."

Luc said nothing.

◆

There was another freak snowfall that afternoon, a foolish thing with the sun shining brightly through the fat snowflakes. It was as if Winter were shaking its fist at Spring, yelling, "I am *so* King of the Castle."

Rodney and John played ball hockey on the driveway in T-shirts and boots. Rodney let a mighty slap shot go, and the ball sailed across the yard and landed near the barn. Retrieving it, Rodney saw footsteps in the mud.

"Did you make the snow angel?" he asked when he came back.

"What snow angel?" said John.

Rodney pointed out the place on the roof where the angel had spread its wings after Thursday's blizzard. You could hardly make it out anymore.

John shook his head solemnly. "Mom would kill me if I went up on the barn roof," he said.

◆

Rodney didn't meet up with Claire on the way to church for evensong. He found her in the changing room already. She was the only one there. Her back was to the door, and she didn't hear him come in. He had been listening to his Walkman. He turned it off, and the tiny click startled Claire out of her wits. She hid something behind her back.

"What are you doing?"

She laid her hand on her chest with relief at seeing it was Rodney. "Quick," she said. "Come and see this before Mrs. Hartwell gets back."

She was holding the black book in which the choirmistress kept notes about this and that and a card of needles, some thread, and a Band-Aid or two. Claire flipped to the back where there was a list of the choir members and their phone numbers. Her finger pointed out the latest entry.

Luc MacEwen, 555-6205.

At first all Rodney saw was that Luc's name was the French spelling. Then he noticed the phone number. It was *his* number. He was aware of Claire's eyes on him. He felt his face growing hot. Neither of them heard Luc enter the room.

"Somebody has a guilty secret," said the new boy, smiling unpleasantly.

Claire immediately slammed the notebook shut and shoved it back into Mrs. Hartwell's handbag.

"Don't *do* that!" she said.

"Do what?" said Luc.

"Sneak up," said Claire.

"You used my phone number," said Rodney.

Luc looked surprised. "That's crazy. Why would I do that?"

"You tell me," said Rodney.

Luc looked from Claire to Rodney a couple of times. It should have been Luc who was caught out. He should have been the one blushing like crazy, but it was the two of them.

Luc shrugged nonchalantly and started to hang up his oversized fringed coat in his locker. "Mrs. Hartwell's an old bag in case you didn't notice," he said. "She must have made a mistake."

"Then what *is* your number?" said Claire.

Luc gathered his music: his hymn and anthem book and psalter. He seemed to think for a moment. "How about 555-5826?" he said.

Claire's chin dropped. "That's *my* number," she said. "How come you know my telephone number?"

A toilet flushed down the hall. They could hear the pipes groan as a tap was turned on.

Luc smiled at her. "A lucky guess." Then Mrs. Hartwell came in. "Shall I tell her?" he said.

"Tell me what?"

But Luc left for the rehearsal room without waiting for an answer.

"Tell me what?" said Mrs. Hartwell. She was a sweet, gruff old lady, devoted to her boys and girls. Claire and Rodney couldn't possibly answer her because then they would have had to admit to rooting around in her purse.

"Nothing," they said simultaneously.

Mrs. Hartwell frowned. She bent down and picked up a card of needles from the floor. "Now, how did these get here?" she said.

In the back hall there was a pay phone. Claire looked through the directory. "McEachern, Mcfadden; there is no McEwen." She looked triumphant.

"Big deal," said Rodney. "He could be from out of town or something." He felt uncomfortable all the same. "Maybe he doesn't have a phone and he was embarrassed, so he just used a number that was already there on the page."

Claire looked at him, unconvinced.

"Well, our numbers are at the top of the page," he said.

Just then Mr. Whithorne called them from the far end of the hall. "Are you two on strike?" he said impatiently.

Claire's eyes flashed. "I don't like this," she said.

◆

It was spring, and the Stanley Cup play-offs were under way, New Jersey against Detroit. As head chorister Rodney sat nearest the congregation at the end of the choir stall. The side of the choir stall rose higher than his head. If he leaned back, he could not be seen by the congregation. That was why he had his Walkman with him. Apart from his duties as head chorister and soloist, he was also the official choir broadcaster of hockey scores during Canon Archibald's brain-numbing sermons.

A finger placed on the red hymnbook represented a score for Detroit; a finger on the black psalter, a score for New Jersey. A finger on the brown Book of Common Prayer meant a penalty to whichever team Rodney indicated by then touching hymnbook or psalter. Touching the anthem book meant there was a brawl! There were a lot of brawls between New Jersey and Detroit.

Claire was head chorister across the chancel from Rodney on the cantoris side. Her job during sermons was to relay the scores back to the kids too far down the choir stalls on Rodney's side — the decani side — to see the original signal. This was important. They didn't want a bunch of decani choirboys leaning forward all the time to see Rodney's signals or Mr. Whithorne would get suspicious. He sat at the organ three rows up behind Claire.

Somebody had explained the code to Luc, but as soon as Rodney started transmitting signals, Luc started sending his own. He didn't seem to care which book he picked up. The kids across the aisle were getting confused. Rodney tried to stop Luc, but that only made him more insistent. There was a lot of whispering on the cantoris side.

"Was that a goal for New Jersey?"

"How could there be a brawl and no penalties?"

The restlessness soon begat fidgeting, which in turn begat commotion. Soon decani kids were leaning forward, looking down the stall towards their head chorister to see what was up.

"Stop it!" said Rodney, wrestling an anthem book away from Luc. Although it was only a whisper, the sizzle of it caught the attention of Mr. Whithorne, who glared over the top of the organ console, trying to spot the culprit. Mr. Whithorne was a master of the full frontal glower. His gaze soon rested on Rodney, whose head sank into the protective confines of the starched high, ruffled collar the choristers wore.

Rodney was furious. It was no use pleading with that glower. Even if he wasn't guilty, he was head chorister. His conduct was expected to be unimpeachable. Eventually Mr. Whithorne's eyebrow lowered, and with one last warning glare he returned to sorting through his sheet music.

But that was not the end of it. Not for Luc. Rodney soon felt a sharp elbow in his side. He shoved back angrily, but Luc only smiled. He had been digging out something from the pocket of his cassock. It was the familiar slim, flat tin of Meloids.

Meloids were a fixture in the choir, but they were strictly forbidden during service. This was because the tins rattled. Luc's rattled now as he emptied several of the hard little pellets into his hand. Rodney didn't dare speak or even move. He was already in enough trouble. He sat bolt upright, eyes ahead, studiously avoiding Luc. Later, he thought, he would strangle Luc and dump his body in the woods for the starving plague-wolves. But for now he was not even going to watch whatever was going to happen next. He did, however, notice Claire's face looking suddenly horror-struck. Then he saw Sean, one of the boys on cantoris, wince and cover his face with his arm.

Rodney dared glance sideways. Luc had made a launch pad of his hymnbook and was flicking Meloids across the aisle at the choristers on the other side. Sean got the first one, Bridgid the second, right on the cheek. She didn't see it coming. "Ow!" she squeaked, and half the choir convulsed in silent laughter. Rodney watched with alarm as

Luc, with deadly accuracy, beaned Claire, right on the nose.

Rodney couldn't take it any longer. Viciously he jabbed Luc in the side. Once, twice. Twisting to avoid the second poke, Luc fired his missile high. The Meloid bounced off the top of the organ console and hit Mr. Whithorne right in the eye.

That eye, blinking and tearing, didn't even look for a culprit this time. Mr. Whithorne pierced Rodney with a laser glower, pinning him to the choir stall.

It was so unfair.

Beside the poor martyr sat Luc, hands folded in his lap, sober as an angel. Mr. Whithorne's finger pointed at Rodney, then pointed over his shoulder to his office down the hall. That is where he would expect Rodney as soon as he had disrobed after the service.

◆

"It's Luc," said Rodney.

"It may well be," said Mr. Whithorne. "He seems a highly spirited lad. But he is *your* responsibility, Rodney."

Mr. Whithorne was washing his eye out at the sink. The Meloid obviously contained some kind of terrible stinging acid. Rodney found himself imagining Mr. Whithorne with a black eyepatch.

"He's not like the other kids, sir."

"How so?"

Rodney wasn't sure what to say. He couldn't talk about the phone number business. Anyway, that wasn't it. It was something in Luc's smile, in the way he did things and the things he said. Something wrong.

"Well?" said the choirmaster, drying his eye with a towel.

Rodney shrugged. "He's sneaky. I don't think he should be in the choir, sir."

"Nonsense, he's just full of beans," said the choirmaster. "A lot of new boys take time to adjust. Besides, I'm sure you've noticed, he has a very good voice."

"He's too loud, sir."

"That can be curbed. He can be trained. But he's got raw talent, Rod. You of all people should recognize that."

Rodney had recognized it all right. He wondered if maybe when he was dumping Luc's strangled body in the woods for the wolves to munch on, it might be a good idea to rip out the corpse's vocal cords while he was at it.

"Well, then?" said Mr. Whithorne. "What have you got to say for yourself?"

Rod took a deep breath. Like Professor Dad, Mr. Whithorne was British and "old school." A statement like "What have you got to say for yourself?" was not an invitation to talk; it was a requisition order for an apology. With great difficulty, Rodney got one out. "I'll try to control him better next time, sir."

"Good lad," said Mr. Whithorne. Then, as he bade Rodney good night, he said, "By the way, the deacon tells me New Jersey is winning going into the third period."

◆

Claire was waiting for him as soon as he left Mr. Whithorne's office. They tromped out into the cool spring night.

"See what I mean?" said Claire.

"Okay, so you were right," said Rodney. "He's a brat."

"Worse than that," said Claire.

"Okay, okay! A complete, screaming pain in the butt," said Rodney.

Then he felt Claire slip her arm through his arm. She'd never done that before. She wanted to speak directly in his ear.

"This afternoon my mother had to help in the church with the altar guild ladies. I came in with her and was hanging around in the sanctuary. And I noticed one of the stained-glass windows. The big one of the archangel Michael standing on Satan's head after the rebellion."

Rodney knew the window, but he looked quizzically at Claire. "What rebellion?"

"The angels' rebellion," she said.

"You mean like Hell's Angels?"

Claire pinched his arm. "Satan was originally an angel. I told you that. Lucifer, the morning star, prince of the fallen angels."

Rodney shook his head. "I just come here to sing," he said.

"Anyway," said Claire, "the window caught my attention. The sun was so bright this afternoon and the light was pouring through it and Michael was all gold and his wings were fiery red. Then I noticed Satan, his hair. Can you remember what he looks like? In the window, I mean."

Rodney tried, but all he could think about was Claire holding his arm, her Meloid-scented breath.

"It's all wavy and long and jet black." Claire paused a moment, waiting for some response from Rodney. "Don't you get it?"

Rodney shook his head. He had no idea what she was talking about. Claire stopped in exasperation and pulled him up short. "You should have gone to Sunday school," she said.

"But I *didn't*," said Rodney, who was fed up. "So just tell me what you're getting at."

"Satan," she said, *"looks just like Luc."*

Rodney tried to remember the face on the church window. "It's just a picture," he said.

"Oh, boy," said Claire. Rodney had never seen her so huffy. "Remember when we first saw him? Remember? How he snuck up behind us? He'd been following us. Following you."

"Yeah, that was pretty weird, but —"

"You just don't get it, do you?" Claire turned away.

"I don't like the guy either," said Rodney. "Why are you so mad at me?"

Finally she turned to face him again. "Because you're not paying attention. His *name*, Rodney," she said. "His name is Luc with a *c*. As in *Lucifer*." She whispered the last bit, hugging his arm tightly.

They walked along in silence in the quietness of a Sunday evening while Rodney tried to absorb what Claire was saying. They had already passed the place where he usually cut off through the woods. He had a feeling that he was walking Claire home. And the awful thing was that he had always wanted to walk her home, but not like this.

"Isn't Luc just the French for Luke?" He tried to

say it as calmly as possible.

Claire stared at him, her eyes large. "You probably don't believe in the devil, do you?" she said.

◆

The path through the woods was sloppy, puddles everywhere. Rodney, in a hurry, slipped more than once. In the deeper darkness he turned on his flashlight. He kept hearing sounds, and he flashed his light this way and that, crazily. He tripped over a root and fell, sprawling in the muck and losing his flashlight. The hoot that followed was no owl.

He lay in the mud, not breathing, waiting to hear it again.

He cursed Claire for what she had said.

The hooting sound came again.

It was human, all right. And it was near.

Then nothing. Nothing but the same wind that moved the wet clouds high above him. What little bit of a moon there was appeared for a sliver of a moment, and in its light Rodney grabbed up his muddy flashlight and climbed to his feet. He rubbed the dirt off his hands, breathing heavily.

"Who is it?" he called.

There was no answer.

By the time he got home, New Jersey had won, big time.

◆

He lay in bed that night trying to sort out the warring sensations of his walk home with Claire. He tried to feel again what it had been like when she held his arm, when her breath was warm in his ear. If only he could drown out what she had been saying.

Tuesday Rodney arrived home from school in time to meet his mother tearing out of the driveway. She stopped the car when she saw him and rolled down her window.

"John's birthday present," she said. "Have you any idea where it is?"

"I don't even know *what* it is," he said. He had bought his brother the usual: a pack of hockey cards, a chocolate bar and an Archie comic.

"A Detroit jersey," said his mother. "An Yzerman jersey. But I can't find it anywhere."

Rodney shook his head. So his mother asked him to help Midge with the birthday cake while she raced downtown to try to get another jersey.

She didn't succeed. There were other hockey sweaters, but there could be no substitute for Yzerman in John's eyes, so she arrived home an hour later with some new Playmobil and a book and scurried upstairs to wrap them in time for dinner.

John liked the Playmobil and the book, but everyone knew what he had been hoping for.

"I'm sorry, honey," said Mrs. Adams. "There just weren't any left." She didn't add "the second time around."

To make matters worse, Detroit lost again that night.

◆

Thursday and choir practice rolled around. The Stanley Cup play-offs were down to the seventh game. With the music festival only two weeks away, Rodney had a solo practice scheduled for the hour before the rest of the choir arrived. He set off for St.

Mike's, munching on a sandwich. The snow was all but gone except for where it lay in hollows shaded from the sun. There was deep snow still piled under the trees near the barn, but none on the roof. The angel was long gone.

Rodney paused. Then he ambled over to the copse of trees where the barn sat and again considered the footsteps there. Snow had melted around them; they were much bigger now. Why hadn't it occurred to him to wonder about this before? Whose footsteps were these? He walked around to the dark side where the trees pressed up close to the building. Someone could have shinnied up one of those trees onto the east-facing side of the roof and then jumped into the deep snow on the west side, leaving no telltale footsteps. Just a perfect angel shape. Any kid passing by on the road might have done it.

Rodney came back around to the big door on the west wall. Being moved on a farmer's flatbed had made the building tilt a bit. The door was hard to open. The big new bolt his mother had put on was stiff.

Holding his sandwich in his teeth, Rodney pried at it. But even as the door finally squeaked open, his mother called to him.

"Rod," she shouted, "get a move on. You've only got fifteen minutes."

Rodney immediately closed the door and set off on his way. With the distraction of his mother calling him, he was already in the woods before his mind registered what his eyes had seen in the barn. In that brief instance when the door opened he had seen in the gloom on the barn floor something that shouldn't have been there: a pizza crust.

◆

O, for the wings, for the wings of a dove.
Far away, far away would I rove.
In the wilderness build me a nest,
And remain there for ever at rest.

Rodney pushed too hard, sang sharp. His breathing was off; he couldn't sustain the long bits. Then on the high G, the second time through, his voice cracked horribly. Two weeks to the music festival, and he was losing it!

Mr. Whithorne patted him on the shoulder and suggested they knock off early. He asked Rodney to go up to the church to get the sheet music of the new anthem they would need for choir practice.

He left Mr. Whithorne playing the piano in the rehearsal studio. He walked along the dim basement hallway with only an echoey murmur of the instrument following him.

Someone was living in the barn. Was the same someone stealing food from their house? There was no one at the Adamses' house all day. The doors were locked, but Rodney remembered his father once having to break in through a basement window because he had forgotten his keys. He had fixed that window, but it had been easy enough to break.

The idea of someone in his house made Rodney shiver. Suddenly a gloomy church basement was the last place he wanted to be. He hurried up the stairs.

His footsteps sounded too loud. His mind was a jumble of grim thoughts: the musty interior of the barn, a pizza crust like a piece of moon, a voice in the woods hooting at him.

He stopped on the landing. Someone was singing in the sanctuary. Rodney climbed on tiptoe to the top of the stairs. It was louder now and the tune was unmistakable.

"O, for the wings of a dove."

From the chancel entranceway Rodney peered around the choir stalls, and there was Luc, standing in the pulpit singing to the empty church. At first all he noticed was the purity of the new boy's voice, the ease with which he nailed each note, the sweet, round vowels, the crispness of the syllables, the sincerity. It was as if he had been singing the song all his life.

But where had he learned it? Eavesdropping, no doubt. Standing outside the rehearsal room, listening.

Then it struck Rodney that Luc was actually standing in the pulpit. Nobody but the minister was supposed to stand in the pulpit.

The singing stopped abruptly. Rodney watched Luc come down the pulpit stairs. He crossed the chancel to the organ console and gathered up some music. Then he saw Rodney.

"Oh, hi," said Luc.

"What are you doing here?" said Rodney.

"I came to pick up Mr. Whithorne's sheet music for him," he said. "Was that what you were after?"

◆

Rodney stood for the longest time, leaning against

the entranceway to the chancel. Long enough for Claire to have to come and fetch him.

"What's up?" she said. "Whithorne's spitting feathers."

"I hate him," said Rodney.

"Whithorne?"

"No!"

Claire didn't need to ask who. "What did he do now?" Her eyes were bright with anticipation. Her voice was filled with a terrible eagerness.

"I *hate* him!" said Rodney.

Claire said nothing. Then she touched his arm. "We'd better get to practice," she said.

Rodney shook her arm away. After a moment Claire left. He heard her slowly descend the stairs at the end of the hall. Her footsteps faded until he was left with only the sound of his heart pounding in his heaving chest.

◆

It was spitting rain by the time he hit the street, raining hard by the time he entered the woods. The trees, winter bare, gave him little protection.

He had arrived eventually for practice, but Mr. Whithorne seemed not to notice him come in. He took his place. Luc was no longer sitting beside him. He was on the cantoris side, standing beside Claire, rubbing shoulders with her. He smiled at Rodney, sweetly.

When practice was over, Rodney left quickly, not wanting to talk to anyone. He wanted nothing more than to go home and change into warm, dry things, make himself a cup of Ovaltine and then settle down with his brother to watch the big game — the last game.

It was pretty clear what was happening. Pretty clear who the someone living in the barn was. He could tell his parents; his parents would contact the police. That was what he should do. The kid was a thief. He would steal anything. He could even steal your voice!

But he had to know for sure. So he made his way to the barn. He had not bolted the door properly. It hung ajar squeaking on its hinges, bumping against the door frame. The barn stood on stout log beams. It was a big step up. Rodney hesitated, then entered.

He stopped and tried to listen through the sound of the rain beating on the tin roof. He took another step, kicked aside the pizza crust. The floorboards were uneven; he tripped and banged his hand against the wall. He put his hand to his mouth and tried to suck out the pain. There was a smell of mildew and mothballs and ancient animal dung.

With his flashlight he surveyed the barn. There were four mangers, each piled high with boxes of secondhand clothing and household articles. Ropes had been strung up between posts to hold winter coats, suits, blouses and skirts. There were skis and skates and records and hot plates and toys — dolls and teddy bears that stared at him with button eyes. Behind a hanging wall of clothing, in the very back of one of the mangers, there was a huge cardboard box in which a stove had once been delivered. Now the box lay on its side. Crouching, Rodney aimed his flashlight into the box.

Something — someone — had hollowed out a nest in the old clothing there. Scraps of food littered the floor around the makeshift bed.

The wind picked up. Now the rain was teeming down on the barn, deafening. The door creaked and banged more loudly against the door frame. Rodney crawled inside the box. He could almost smell him here. There was a ratty old fur coat that looked as if it had been used as a blanket. Under its corner, Rodney saw red. He threw back the coat. There lay a brand-new Detroit hockey jersey with a C for Captain on the front and *Yzerman* in red letters on the back.

Rodney felt his pulse pounding in his ears. He picked up the jersey. His heart was racing.

Then, suddenly, the door to the barn slammed shut, followed by the rasping sound of the bolt sliding home.

Clutching the hockey jersey, Rodney crawled under the hanging wall of coats, clambered to his feet and picked his way to the door through the cluttered dark. It was the wind, he told himself; he prayed it was the wind. But the wind cannot press home a stiff new bolt! Even through the rattling of the rain on the roof he could hear the laughter outside. He tried the door. It was locked.

"Let me out!"

Nothing.

"Let me out, Luc. Please!"

He waited. Panic-stricken.

"This isn't funny!" he yelled, and his voice cracked.

He pushed on the door. He leaned his back against it, heaving with all his might. It would not budge. He stopped to catch his breath. His flashlight beam flew around the walls of the barn like a trapped bird. There was no other exit, no windows. He could call for help, but no one in the house would hear him.

Maybe there was a tool to pry open the door. Or a saw. He looked for a saw, but his imagination would not let him search in peace. The dark was filled with menacing shadows.

He tried to fight off his fear. He would just wait out the rain. Someone would come looking for him. He had to stay calm. He slid down to the floor.

He cleared his throat and tried to hum, but his voice was broken. Totally. He knew it. His solo days were over. His head drooped on his chest. Then his eyes glimpsed something curling through the beam of his flashlight.

Smoke. Smoke was coming up through the floor-boards.

"Oh, God," he said. "Oh, no."

Suddenly there was a cry outside. Thumping sounds. Another cry.

"Who's there?" he yelled. "Help!"

He listened, pressed his ear hard to the door, heard noises moving off into the bush.

"No, no. Come back," he cried, pounding on the door. "Get me out of here!" His voice was in shreds now. He started to cough. Smoke filled the barn.

Then someone was at the door. He leaped back, grabbing the first thing that came to hand, a china lamp. He heard grunting. The bolt outside flew back. He gripped the lamp tightly in both hands and raised it high, his flashlight between his knees aimed at the doorway to blind his adversary.

The door swung open. A shadowy figure covered its face against the light. He started to swing. Stopped.

It was Claire. She was soaked in mud, her hair wet and tangled, her forehead bleeding. She reached up, grabbed him by the arm and dragged him out of the barn.

"What's going on?" cried Rodney.

Breathless, she leaned against the barn and pointed down. Between the log beams under the doorway, a fire of twigs and rags was already licking the floorboards of the barn.

Rodney threw aside the lamp, found a long branch and, on his knees, dragged the burning matter out into the open, where the rain made it hiss and the smoke made them both cough. Claire found a shovel somewhere and joined in. Finally, the job done, they stood limp and exhausted, letting the rain beat down on them.

"He was following you," said Claire, gulping for air. "I followed him into the woods. When I caught up with him, he had already set the fire."

She pushed wet hair out of her face, and Rodney gently pulled her inside the door out of the rain. They sat together on the threshold of the barn. The door was flung wide open. They weren't taking any chance that he might come back.

Rodney put his arms around her and hugged her. She held on tightly.

"You saved my life," he said.

She looked at him with a worried look on her face. "Your voice," she said.

He could only smile weakly. "Singing isn't everything," he said.

♦

They made their way back to the house, soaked and reeking of smoke. Professor Dad found a padlock and quickly went to put it on the shed door. Mother found dry clothes and made phone calls. Midge made tea for everyone.

The Yzerman jersey was rain-soaked by now, but all the better a present, as far as John was concerned, for the story that came with it. Before his mother could stop him, he put it on and scampered up to watch the final period of the hockey game.

No one followed. Professor Dad lit a fire, and they sat around in the living room, waiting for Claire's parents. But John soon joined them again. He raced downstairs, thumping and clumping the whole way and screeching like a banshee.

The game was over. The Wings had won.

THE PINHOLE CAMERA

At the foot of Ford's bed there was a hole that led to another world. Milo was the first to find it. He always jumped up on the bed, kneaded Ford's chest with his claws and demanded to be allowed under the covers. Ford lifted the covers, and Milo would tunnel to the end of the bed, where he would scratch and dig and meow.

"Isn't twelve a bit old for this kind of thing?" said Ford's mother. She was choosing clothes for him to wear to school.

Ford had the covers over his head. He was staring down past his feet to where Milo was clawing away.

His mother gently pulled the covers off his head.

"Too old for what?" he asked.

"Other worlds," said his mother wearily.

"Well, if I have to choose between this world and the other one," he said, pulling the covers back over his head, "then I guess I'll stay in here."

Milo was facing him, his golden eyes gleaming in the dark. Now another idea crowded the hole out of Ford's mind for the time being. This dark under the covers was all that was left of the night.

"Hey, cool!" he said, clamping the bedclothes down around him to trap the night. Milo purred.

He liked the night. Better hunting.

"Now what?" said his mother.

"Leftover night," he said through the covers. "You never know when it might come in handy."

His mother tugged the covers off him again. Less gently.

Ford sat up. "Okay, okay," he said huffily. "But if I'm too old for other worlds, aren't I a bit old for you to pick out my clothes for me?"

His mother relented. "Just don't take forever," she said as she went downstairs.

Ford leaned back against the headboard. Milo joined him.

"What if I took Forever, Milo..." he said, scratching the cat behind the ears. "I mean, if I *stole* Forever. What would people do without it?"

◆

At the foot of Ford's street there was a shortcut to school. The path, its entrance almost entirely overgrown, led through woodland along a stream for a bit, up a steep hill to a high meadow overgrown with grasses and wildflowers. Beyond a wall of scruffy-looking bushes there was another steep hill down to a deep, litter-strewn ditch and then the parking lot of a doughnut place.

Ford had mapped this country, and on his map it was the Tumbling Forest. The stream was Gibberish Creek, and as for the field, as pretty as it appeared in bloom and as fragrant as it smelled, it could not hide the ugly truth that lay rotting beneath it. For this was the Field of the Two Gladiators, named in honour of a bloody conflict fought there in ancient times. Ford had excavated armour parts and had piled them up with some bloodstained rocks into a noble-looking monument, a soldier made of stone, metal and wood, standing on guard at the edge of the meadow. Ford had been late for school that day. A monument cannot be rushed.

The school guidance counsellor, Mr. Poole, had a talk with him. It wasn't the first time Ford had been late.

"How are you liking Westdale, Ford?"

"It's okay."

"Have you made any friends?"

Ford thought for a moment. He looked at Mr. Poole's perky face set off by a very perky red polka-dot bow tie. Mr. Poole was a Good Listener, and Ford appreciated a Good Listener. But in the end he decided not to tell the counsellor about the Society of Feathered Tumblers — SOFT, for short — who lived in the Tumbling Forest. Part of him thought that Mr. Poole might enjoy hearing about the adventures of such a knockabout company of pranksters, but another part of him was pretty sure that the story would only bring about more counselling. Maybe even a shrink. Ford had been to see a shrink in the last place they lived. Shrinks were a pain because that was what they did. They tried to shrink you — or, at least, shrink your world until it was the same size as everybody else's.

"One size fits all."

"What's that?"

Ford hadn't meant the words to leak out. "Juan Diaz and Terry Fitzall," he said. "They don't go here. I met them at the pool."

Mr. Poole looked happy; his bow tie looked

happy. "Good," he said. "But what about joining one of the school clubs? Drama, maybe — an imaginative kid like you."

"Okay," said Ford. "The drama club might be a good idea." Or how about the Brotherhood of the Heathen Rule? he thought. The highest order of the Society of Feathered Tumblers. You had to be invited to become a member, and the initiation was gruelling but he was just about ready to make the step.

Poole was staring at him in an odd, expectant way. Ford smiled. This time he was sure nothing had slipped out. His mouth was clamped shut.

◆

"In trouble again?"

It was Woody Sparks. He sat next to Ford in art class. Ford was late for school again. This was the first time Woody had ever spoken to him. Woody didn't talk much to anyone. He was strange. Not strange looking, exactly. But he acted strangely. He blinked a lot and looked kind of lost and surprised, as though he had just emerged from the primordial swamp and didn't know what was going on.

"Not exactly trouble," Ford whispered as soon as Ms. Dillard's back was turned. "It's just my dog."

"You have a dog?"

"Messerschmitt," said Ford. "He attacked somebody."

Woody looked interested in a nervous kind of way, as if maybe Ford had his dog on him somewhere and it might be better to sink down again into the dark, protective ooze.

"It attacked somebody?"

"An old lady," said Ford. "Maimed her for life."

Now Woody was all sticky-outy ears and popping eyes.

"This is the third time," said Ford dramatically.

"No way," said Woody. Then suddenly a tug-of-war broke out on his face. It was as if some of his facial muscles still wanted to express astonishment, while others didn't believe Ford's story one bit. Ford watched with downright amazement. Woody's face was out of control! Then Woody dropped his eyes and turned away, embarrassed at being tricked.

Ford didn't have any friends, but he was new in town. He had an excuse. Woody had lived in Westdale all his life, as far as Ford knew. He didn't have any friends because he was obviously demented.

That's all I need, thought Ford. A demented friend. So he turned away from Woody Sparks. Let him sink back into the dark.

◆

Ford never saw anyone in the Tumbling Forest, but sometimes he thought he heard voices. He always ducked out of sight. He didn't want to have to explain what he was doing there. There weren't any signs saying Private Property, Keep Off, Trespassers Will Be Executed, or anything like that. But he always felt as if he weren't supposed to be there. That made it kind of exciting and dangerous. As long as you didn't get caught.

More than once he even thought he heard someone singing. It happened again after school, on the same day that he captured and set free the leftover night and wondered out loud to Milo about stealing

Forever. He dived into the bushes. The singing seemed to stop. Cautiously he poked his head up to look around. He didn't see anyone.

"It was just Gibberish Creek," he muttered to himself. "Chattering away, luring another woodland animal to its doom." He liked this idea. The first wizard of SOFT taught the creek to talk like that, he thought, in order to charm creatures to its shore, where the Tumblers could trap them, especially the birds, whose feathers they could use to make their costumes.

"That's all I'm hearing," said Ford. "It's spring. The creek's got a lot to talk about."

Then he heard it again. Singing. And that bothered him. It made him wonder if maybe the singing was in his head. Hearing voices in your head was not the same as making things up. Ford knew that.

♦

Ford liked art. It was the only thing at school he enjoyed. So he was disappointed a few days later to find Ms. Dillard away. He had let her in on the Tumbling Forest and was hoping to tell her about his latest adventures there.

Woody Sparks came up for air long enough to express disappointment as well. "I hope she's not in any trouble," he said, glancing tentatively at Ford.

Ford looked straight at him, and Woody kind of shrivelled like a leaf under a magnifying glass.

"What is it with you and trouble?" Ford asked him.

Woody didn't answer.

The substitute, who had been drawing on the blackboard, turned around and cleared his throat for attention.

He was in a black suit and a black tie. He looked like an undertaker. Especially his face. He looked as if his face had been left out in the rain too long and had rusted into a perpetual frown.

Ms. Dillard had dancing eyes. She was the kind of teacher you could actually talk to about things, about SOFT even, though usually she would interrupt Ford excitedly and say things like "No, Ford, don't tell me, show me. Paint the Tumblers. Don't leave out the slightest detail."

The substitute didn't look like an art teacher at all, certainly not the kind who would let you use any colours you liked.

His voice was deep, sombre. "My name is Thorogood. I am going to be with you for...a while."

"I bet he killed Dillard," said Woody Sparks under his breath.

Ford shot a glance at Woody. He had been thinking exactly the same thing.

"We are going to make a camera," said Mr. Thorogood. "A pinhole camera."

Toys, thought Ford, disgusted.

On the board the undertaker had drawn detailed plans of how they were to construct the camera out of a single flat piece of black cardboard that they would fold into the shape of a small box.

"When it is utterly lightproof," he said, "I will give each of you one of these." He held up a small black envelope between his thumb and index finger as if he were holding a squirming critter by the tail. "In this package is a single piece of photosensitive paper, which each of you will place in your camera.

You will do this at home, in the dark."

Ford sat up a little straighter in his chair.

"No light must touch the emulsion on the surface of this paper until the very moment when you have chosen a fitting subject and, holding your camera perfectly still, you remove the protective flap covering the pinhole and commit your subject matter to Immortality."

◆

It was stuffy in the closet and a bit scary, even though Ford had made it as comfortable as possible. He had dragged in a chair and arranged himself with the camera and the package of light-sensitive paper on his lap, and a glue stick in his breast pocket, and black duct tape on his wrist like a bracelet. He had closed the door and covered over the crack of light along the bottom with his dressing gown.

He waited the way you wait in the dark until the shapes of things around you become apparent. But even after a full minute he could see nothing. It was perfectly dark.

Milo scratched at the door, and Ford jumped out of his skin.

"Go away," he said.

Milo meowed plaintively.

Ford was sweating. He didn't mind the dark under his covers, but this dark was different — all tight and closed-in feeling.

Milo scratched again.

"Get lost!" he shouted.

He wiped the sweat out of his eyes, wiped his hand on his pants leg and then gingerly pulled the photosensitive paper from its lightproof envelope, holding it by the edges. You had to glue the paper to the inside back of the camera, then fit the front panel of the box — the one with the pinhole in it — securely, wrapping the edges with a ton of duct tape so that no light could get in.

"Ford?"

Oh, great. It was his mother. "I'm in my room," he yelled. "Don't come in!"

Then he heard her coming up the stairs. Milo meowed and scratched at the closet door again.

"Thanks a lot, buddy," said Ford.

"Ford? Where are you?"

He put the front of the camera in place. With anxious fingers he made certain that the cardboard gate over the pinhole was secure, that it hadn't been knocked off in the dark. Then he tore off a piece of the duct tape with his teeth and began wrapping it around the edge of the camera as quickly as he could, pressing it down all around.

His bedroom door opened.

"Ford?"

He tore off another piece of duct tape with his teeth and covered over the tape he had just put down.

"Don't come in," he said.

But it was too late. The closet door opened, and the light blinded him.

"What are you doing?"

He didn't answer. As soon as his eyes adjusted, he frantically examined the camera. His tape work wasn't pretty, but it looked functional, at least. No holes.

"What is that?"

Ford held it up for his mother's inspection. "It's a trap," he said.

She immediately backed off. "You've caught something in there?"

Ford beamed. "Not yet," he said.

◆

But he knew what he wanted. The sun was already in the west, but the sky was cloudless, and the light was fine. Ford's monument would look pretty impressive right about now.

He made his way quickly through the Tumbling Woods along Gibberish Creek towards the Field of the Two Gladiators. He was almost there when he heard the singing.

He stopped in his tracks. He looked around. No one. He shook his head. It wouldn't go away. He listened some more.

I'm going crazy, he thought.

But it was real. It was high up. In the trees? He scanned the branches. No. Suddenly he was frightened, but there was no time to hide or wait. The light would not last, and the picture was due tomorrow.

He climbed the rocky path that led up from the streambed to the edge of the field. The singing got louder. It was coming from the Field of the Two Gladiators.

It was Woody Sparks.

He was just standing there, up to his knees in wildflowers, singing. It was no song Ford recognized. He seemed to be making it up as he went along.

At the shock of seeing him there, it took Ford a

moment to register what else Woody was up to. Not until the instant he bent his head down as if in prayer did Ford notice the cardboard box in the boy's hands. And the monument a few paces away.

"Stop!" he cried, breaking from the trees.

Woody almost leaped out of his skin.

"What do you think you're doing?" screamed Ford. "That's mine."

Woody's face was going haywire. "You ruined it!" he shouted back at Ford. "You ruined my picture."

Ford stopped short, a shadow's length away. He was breathing hard. "Good!" he said. "It's my statue. Get lost."

Woody had been staring down sadly at his pinhole camera. Now his head jerked up. "Yours? Are you crazy?" His voice cracked with emotion. "That thing over there?"

Ford nodded.

"Ha!" said Woody. "As if."

Ford's face grew red with anger. "I built it."

"Ha!" said Woody again. "It was built by aliens."

Ford was stunned. "You really are demented," he said. "Aliens?"

Woody nodded gravely. He looked as if he were going to go on, but he stopped himself.

"Tell me about it," Ford demanded.

Woody stared hard at Ford, then took a deep breath. "A saucer crashed here, and the survivors built it as a monument to their comrades who didn't make it."

Ford looked at the statue. "Not bad," he said, "but *wrong*."

"Well, what is it supposed to be?" said Woody. So Ford told him.

"Gladiators?"

"Look a bit closer," said Ford. "See the shields?"

Woody shook his head. "I see heat deflectors. And that thing that looks like a spine is an axle. What kind of gladiator has an axle?"

Ford stared dumbfounded at Woody. "What kind of flying *saucer* has an axle?" he shouted.

Then neither of them spoke.

They both turned to look at the monument. The sun had slipped down behind the wall of trees, and the monument was plunged into dimness. Now it looked more like a scrap heap than anything else. Just so many hubcaps and head lamps and rusted engine parts.

"This is my property," said Ford, his voice low and warning.

But Woody didn't budge. He didn't look frightened the way he did in class. He had left the swamp behind. His eyes didn't skitter away from contact.

"Nobody owns Parasilva."

"Parawhat?"

Woody folded his arms on his chest. "I am the protector of this place. The people of Xchon will be returning here from their planet. They have left me in charge. I will not betray them."

Ford chortled. "Oh, that's a good one," he said. Then he turned and headed back towards the woods. But he turned and spoke again as threateningly as he could. "Just wait until SOFT hears about this."

"Who's soft?" cried Woody, his voice wavering a bit.

Ford heard the uncertainty in his voice. "You'll find out," he said, "if you ever set foot in the Tumbling Woods again."

◆

When he got home, there was someone sitting at the kitchen table, talking to his mother. A stranger.

"Ford, this is Martha Lunberg. She not only works at the same office as I do, but guess what? We just realized today she lives around the corner. Small world, isn't it?"

Ford shook hands with Martha Lunberg. She had a nice smile.

"We've decided to carpool," said Martha.

"Cool," said Ford, and he turned to go up to his room.

"I was just telling Martha about your pinhole camera."

"Did you get your picture?" asked Martha.

Ford looked at her and shook his head. "Somebody had already taken it," he said.

Martha Lunberg seemed to find this hysterically funny. "Somebody had already taken it," she said. "What a comedian." Ford watched his mother's face light up, glad to hear that someone found her son ha-ha funny instead of just weird funny.

◆

When his mother came up to say good-night, Ford said, "Looks like you've got yourself a friend."

His mother shrugged, but there was a satisfied look on her face. "Only time will tell," she said.

When she was gone, Ford thought, But who will Time tell? Will he blab it all over the place? Or does Time have a particular friend he tells stuff to?

♦

Ford was up first thing without his mother having to prod him. So was the sun. He was out of the house early. He still needed a photograph for Mr. Thorogood, and since Woody Sparks had stolen his subject matter, he wasn't sure what else to do.

But it didn't take long to find the perfect thing. The entrance to the shortcut at the end of the block was pierced by morning sunlight. As overgrown as it was, the way stood open like a magic doorway with a golden carpet of spring sun leading down into the cool shadows.

He bent over his little box, holding it as still as possible. It wasn't like a normal camera. There was no viewfinder to look through, no knob to focus, no film to wind. You took aim and just imagined the picture you were taking. When he was ready, Ford peeled back the cover from the pinhole.

"One thousand and one," he said. Then he covered up the hole again. Too much light would destroy it.

♦

The picture was a bit of a surprise. It was fuzzy, for one thing. And black and white. Thorogood had warned them that the pictures would be black and white, but nobody in the class had been ready for it. Some people were disappointed, but when he got used to it, Ford wasn't. It made it seem more special somehow. Real but unreal. It was a great picture.

And so was Woody Spark's. When Ford had shouted at him in the high meadow, he had just managed to get the cover back over his pinhole in time, before losing it.

The class was especially knocked out by Woody's picture. Woody wasn't used to so much attention, but he seemed pleased by it.

"It's spooky," someone said.

"Kind of bad-looking," said someone else.

"As in menacing?" suggested Mr. Thorogood.

"Yeah, menacing."

"Did you build that guy?" someone asked.

He shook his head, looking shyly at Ford. "Ford built it," he said. "It's a gladiator."

"Excellent," said someone.

People were really impressed.

"Where is that place?" someone asked.

Ford went cold all over, but before he could say anything, Woody started describing how to get there. It was a good description, very detailed, except for one important feature. It was totally made up. A complete lie. The secret location of the Field of the Two Gladiators was safe.

Ford gave Woody a secret thumbs-up.

As they were leaving class, Mr. Thorogood called Ford back. "While the subject matter of Woody's piece is striking, I have to say, Ford, that your picture is my favourite, compositionally."

They looked at the photo mounted on the corkboard among the others. It did stand out. It was brighter, for one thing.

"Captured like that in full morning light, the pathway seems to beckon the viewer to enter a magic kingdom," said Mr. Thorogood.

◆

This story could have ended like that. Or with Ford showing his mother the photograph and telling her that this was the other world he'd been talking about and her saying, "Whoa! This is at the end of your bed? I'd better change your sheets more often." Or something like that.

But if it had ended there, you wouldn't know what happened the next day. You wouldn't know about Ford and Woody's final confrontation.

It was Saturday. Heavy clouds. Rain on and off. Ford slept in, watched cartoons, read a couple of old *Tintins*, then messed around in the basement with a computer he'd dug out of someone's garbage to see if he could make anything out of it. Around three, bored out of his skull, he thought about phoning Woody Sparks just to say thanks for not giving away where the monument was.

Mrs. Sparks answered in a cheery voice. "Woody's not in right now," she said. "He's off on some secret mission to somewhere called Parasilva."

Ford was off like a shot. The rain had stopped for the time being, but it was cool in the Tumbling Woods, unusually gloomy but alive with wind that shook the rain out of the trees. Ford was drenched in a matter of moments. Drenched and shivering. The Society of Forest Tumblers were nowhere to be seen. They hated getting their feathers wet. They didn't much like the wind, either; they *really* hated getting their feathers ruffled.

Ford found himself a stout man-sized stick. There might be trouble. He might have to drive a certain somebody back into the primordial sludge.

The wind was almost gale force on the Field of the Two Gladiators. But that's where Woody was, and he wasn't alone. He was surrounded by a squadron of balloons.

He was singing, but the wind grabbed up his words, shredded them and flung them around. It was impossible to say what he might be singing about. Balloons, thought Ford. There were about a dozen of them so far, all bright yellow, fluttering above the boy's head, tethered by long strings to a large rock. Woody was squatting, filling them up with a small compressor.

When he looked up, finally, his eyes took in the stick Ford was holding and he tensed up a little, but he didn't show any signs of leaving. Not even when Ford held up the stick threateningly.

"I don't think this place belongs to anybody." Woody had to shout to be heard above the wind. He sounded nervous but defiant. "I don't know who SOFT is, but I'm not scared of him."

A gust of wind bashed the balloons around. They looked lively enough to take on anything.

Ford let go of one end of the stick, held it like a staff, not a weapon. Woody seemed to relax a little.

He filled up another balloon. When it was good and fat, Ford noticed him shoving something in the end before making the knot.

He came closer. "What are you putting in them?"

"Helium," said Woody. "To make them go farther."

"No, no, that," said Ford. "The rolled-up thing. Is it a note?"

Woody nodded.

"Is this how you communicate with the people of Shon?" said Ford.

Woody stood up, pushed the hair out of his eyes. "It's Xchon, with an *X*." He looked warily at Ford and shook his head. "I don't think even with helium in it a balloon could travel thirty thousand light-years."

Ford nodded. "That's what I was wondering." He looked back towards the line of trees that marked the entrance to the Tumbling Woods. He imagined the Feathered Tumblers hiding behind those trees, watching him, expecting him to drive this trespasser away. He felt like a defector even listening to talk about Xchon. This was the Field of the Two Gladiators, not Parasilva. That's probably what the Tumblers were saying — yelling at him right now.

"Throw the bum out! The Feathered Tumblers demand the hide of this intruder!"

But there were no voices. Not that you could hear. They'd be safe at home in weather like this. Too much wind. So Ford turned his back on the forest and squatted down. It wasn't nearly so blustery if you hunkered down low in the grass.

Woody was on his knees, shoving a rolled-up note into a balloon. After he had tied it off and attached it to the string, Ford handed him another balloon from the bag lying on the ground.

Woody thanked him, dug out one of the notes from his pocket and handed it to him to read.

The note said, "Hi, my name is Woody Sparks." Then it gave his address.

Ford rolled it up tightly the way he had seen Woody do it and handed it to the boy.

"I heard about some kids in Detroit doing this

and the balloons went all over, as far as New York State even."

Ford's face filled with wonder. "Really?"

"Really," said Woody. "I came up here because it's the best place for blastoff."

"You're right about that," said Ford. The wind was whistling around his ears. But when he looked up, he couldn't help wondering if anything could break through such an oppressive cloud cover.

Woody sat on the wet ground and leaned back on his hands. He had finished the bag of balloons. Two dozen. What a sight they were, bumping and thumping around, straining at their tethers. He looked expectantly at Ford. "Well, here goes nothing."

Then he pushed the rock away, and the balloons leaped into the air, twirling and shooting this way and that and rising into the turbulent sky.

Ford had to stand up and cheer. It just jumped out of him, a big yellow balloon of applause. Woody looked pleased with himself. He cheered, too.

"Who knows how far they'll go?" he shouted.

They chased the balloons. They yelled at them, Ford swinging at them with his stick. "Get moving, you lazy balloons. Get outa here. Shoo! Shoo!"

When they were tired out, they just watched, their necks bent way back, until all the balloons had blown right off that high wild meadow — whatever its name was. They watched until the last one disappeared from sight. It had seemed to defy the winds and risen straight up into the clouds, higher and higher, shining like a miniature sun. When it was very high, Ford squinted and it seemed like a hole into the darkness. A hole that led to somewhere bright.

THE CHINESE BABIES

"Here's what you need to know. Be open."

Molly's grandfather leaned over the chessboard, his hand hovering here, there, shaking a little. Finally she watched his waxy, yellow-tipped fingers descend on a bishop and slide him all the way over to the left side of the board. Any minute now he would tell her the name of that square.

"Queen's bishop to king's rook six."

There. She didn't know why he did this. She was twelve now. He'd been doing it since she was seven, and she *still* didn't know which square was which or why they should have numbers.

And what had he said about being open? Quickly she checked to make sure her queen wasn't trapped. She wasn't. Her regal eyes were flinty, on guard. She could move all right. Her hubby, the king, was tucked up all nice and safe behind a wall of pawns with a knight by his side. Even with all that protection, he still looked scared. What a wuss.

This was the only strategy Molly knew. Keep the wuss-king out of the way and the flinty-eyed queen loose and ready to attack.

Be open?

Molly's eyes roamed the board. Everything looked fine.

Grandfather leaned back in his La-Z-Boy rocker. "I always felt sorry for that foolish duck," he said.

Molly stared at her grandfather, looked down at the board, expecting to see a duck there. She examined the bishop he had just moved, wondering if maybe the bishop was a duck in disguise.

"You know, Molly, maybe that's why I've always loved the oboe." Grandfather's fingers were tapping lightly on the arm of his chair, to some rhythm Molly couldn't hear. Ducks? Oboes? What was he up to?

"What about the oboe, Taid?"

"Hmm?"

"Why do you love the oboe?"

"Oh," said her grandfather, as if Molly had asked him a truly challenging question. "Well, because of the duck," he said. "Getting swallowed by the wolf and all. Such a bad business that..."

Mum sometimes said Grandfather Gareth was losing it. She called him Taid, which was Welsh for grandfather. "Taid Gareth is getting senile, Molly. He's starting to dodder a bit." Was this what she meant?

Molly waited. Waiting was a pretty good strategy with Taid Gareth. And while she waited, she examined the chessboard. Ah-ha! Her castle was right across the board from the shaky old bishop. No wonder he was praying so hard!

She was just about to slide her castle across the board and bump the old bishop off when Grandfather piped up again. "It's funny how you can know something all your life and not ever really know how it came to be."

Molly's head was spinning. Playing chess with her grandfather was difficult enough without all this doddering. She didn't wait for him to go on. With a satisfying clink, Molly took her grandfather's bishop. She hit the chess piece so hard it bounced right off the game table and landed on the dog's nose. The dog woke up.

"Sorry, Blossom," said Molly.

Blossom nosed the bishop with his big wet nose. Licked him. Poor bishop. Molly swooped the piece up before Blossom made a lunch of him. She put him into the chess box. She called the chess box Heaven. There were three of Grandfather's pawns there already. She hardly ever won an important piece off Grandfather.

She turned the four pieces so that they were facing each other, so that they could have a little chat. Otherwise Heaven was a pretty boring place.

She turned her attention back to the board in time to see Taid Gareth lift one of his castles and move it slowly all the way from his end of the board, past the square where her castle had been, right to her end of the board, behind her defence and only three squares away from the wuss-king's backside.

"Rook to queen's rook eight," said Taid Gareth.

"Queen's *castle* eight," said Molly grumpily.

Grandfather smiled wickedly at her. "Check," he said.

Molly was just about to slide old Flinty-Eyes between Wuss-King and the marauding Black Castle when she realized that she couldn't. If she moved her queen, she would automatically be in check from Grandfather's other castle.

"And checkmate," said Grandfather with satisfaction, licking his parched lower lip. The gleam in his eye didn't look very senile.

"You got me with just your castles," she said.

"Rooks," said Grandfather, chuckling, dry as dust. "You can call them castles all you like, Molly fach, but that makes them sound inactive. Just sitting there, doing nothing."

Molly wasn't a good loser, but she had learned how to be a quiet loser. Taid Gareth had taught her all about buttoning your lip when you didn't like what was going on. She glared at him one good solid glare, then started putting her players back in the box.

"So what is a rook anyway?" she asked.

"Well," said her grandfather, "there's one kind of rook that is a bird, kind of like a raven. Did you see how silently it flew down your flank there and caught you off guard?"

Molly put Taid's players away while he loaded up his pipe. "Yeah, well, how was I supposed to notice with you talking all the time?"

Taid Gareth reached across and rebuttoned her lips. His eyes wrinkled up. "I tried to warn you," he said. "Remember? Be open."

Molly had the two black rooks in each hand. She made them caw angrily at each other.

Her grandfather laughed. "The rook in chess comes from the Persian word for warrior," he said.

Molly plopped the two victorious warriors back in the box, slid the top closed and put the chess box into the drawer under the game table.

"What about the duck?" she said.

Her grandfather was leaning back now, staring past her at the great white expanse of sloping yard and wide frozen river and distant hills that the view from this room afforded him. "From *Peter and the Wolf*," he said. "You have heard it, haven't you?"

This was a trick question. He had given her a tape of *Peter and the Wolf* last year for Christmas. She had never listened to it. "Oh, that duck," she said.

Grandfather sucked on his pipe, seemingly unaware of her fib. "My favourite instrument in the orchestra has been the oboe for as long as I can recall. But I don't like the clarinet worth a hoot. Now, that's silly, really. They're not all that much different. But I like the oboe, Molly fach."

Molly curled up on the floor so that her head was snuggled against Blossom's woolly neck.

"And it's all because of the duck?" she said, her voice muffled by Blossom fuzz.

Taid Gareth nodded. "As you'll recall, in Mr. Prokofiev's story, the duck's part is played by the oboe. Such a plaintive sound, you see. The poor old duck never did get out of the wolf."

Blossom licked Molly's ear. She nuzzled deeper into his warm, smelly pelt to escape this wet gesture.

"Not even in the sequel?" she asked.

"The sequel?"

"Isn't there a sequel?" said Molly. "*Return of the Duck* or something like that?"

Grandfather chuckled. "We didn't go in for sequels much in my day. We were lucky if we got something once."

Molly uncoiled herself from Blossom and made her way over to the official scoreboard by the study door. THE ANNUAL WIGSTEAD CHRISTMAS CHESS TOURNAMENT, the sign read. With a black Magic Marker Molly recorded her loss, Gareth's win.

"Luckily there's a sequel in the tournament," she said. "I'll get you yet, Taid."

There were eight of them at the old Wigstead farm for Christmas. Taid Gareth; Molly, her mother, Charlotte, and her father, Trick; Aunt Estelle and her boyfriend, Chet; and Uncle Don, the oldest, and his sixteen-year-old son, Keith.

After round one, Grandfather Gareth was on top with six wins and only one loss, a fluke to Chet. "He's just trying to make you feel wanted," Estelle told him. "He'll clobber you next time."

When it came to chess, Taid Gareth was merciless.

Charlotte was next with five wins. Then Chet, who was tied for third spot with Estelle.

Molly was next with three wins, tied with her dad. With one round left, she could still win. Well, maybe not against her grandfather, but then he played all the time. He played by mail with friends back in Wales and some missionary in Africa.

Trailing the pack were Uncle Don and Keith. Keith had won zero games. He had lost six in a row. After two complete rounds everyone should have played seven games, but Don and Keith's game was declared a draw. It wasn't really a draw. With one angry swipe, Uncle Don cleared the table in the middle of their game. He sent the players flying every which way. He was making a point to Keith about something. Nobody knew exactly what. Then Don went out for a while, and Molly, silently, helped Keith recover the chess pieces. One of the points on the white king's crown was broken. Trick secretly took the injured king out to Grandfather's workshop in the garage and sanded it smooth. "Poor old wuss-king," Molly said, as she watched her father working. Her mother came out to the shed to see how things were going.

She was fuming. "I can't believe this childish behaviour between those two," she said.

Molly huffed. "When someone's as old as Uncle Don, shouldn't it be called adultish behaviour?"

◆

This was the first Christmas Keith had been there since Grandmother Maeve had died. Don got Keith for Christmas only every other year. Nain Maeve had always been able to smooth things out between Don and his son. Molly missed her.

So, while everyone else was relatively happy and enjoying a few days up at the old Wigstead homestead, Don and Keith took turns walking out along the Old Bridge Road or down to the riverside.

That's where Keith was when Molly curled up in the study after lunch the day of her defeat to Taid Gareth.

It was snowing. Keith was down at the river's edge, smoking a cigarette. The cigarettes were the cause of the first big fight of the holidays. Don was furious, blamed it all on Montreal, where Keith lived with his mother. They had moved there three years ago. Don hadn't liked the idea, and Taid Gareth had sided with him. "There's only one thing wrong with Quebec, and that's the French," Grandfather Gareth had said.

"Silly old fart," Charlotte said, making Molly laugh. Then she felt bad. She loved her grandfather, even if she didn't like all the things he said.

Molly was kneeling at the picture window. Blossom was asleep by the fireplace. He twitched, farted.

"Silly old fart," murmured Molly, but not loudly enough to wake the dog. She didn't want his sloppy attention right now. Her eyes fixed on her only cousin, Keith. He was so quiet, so moody. She watched him walk out onto the river. The ice was thick this year and covered with an eiderdown of deep snow. There was a crust so you could walk on top of the snow, although sometimes your foot went through.

Mum had taken her out on the snowmobile, all the way across to the other side. That was Quebec over there, those low hills. Before the Trans-Canada Highway had been built, the old highway that passed the Wigstead place had led to a bridge upriver a bit that hopped several islands right over to the other side. The bridge wasn't there anymore, but the road was still called the Old Bridge Road. There was a barn up the road from Grandfather's house, near the highway, that had some writing on the side. "Pont d'Entente," it read in peeled and weather-beaten letters.

Molly thought it was sad that the bridge was gone. The great square stone pylons were still there, solid as ever, but they looked kind of stupid without something to hold up.

Mum had taken Molly upriver on the snowmobile, and they drove from pylon to pylon across the ice, just as if they were crossing over on a memory.

Keith was standing way out on the ice now. There was a wind out there blowing his shirttails around. He wouldn't wear a coat. That was fight number two with Uncle Don.

"Maybe your mother lets you walk around naked in sub-zero weather, but you'll wear a coat while you're up here."

It was as if the two of them were having their own private Wigstead tournament. Except that no one was winning.

Blossom sighed, content in some fire-warmed dream. But Molly was getting worried about Keith. The ice was thick, sure, but they had always been told how dangerous it was to be out too far on the river alone. There were fast currents where the ice only set thick enough to hold the weight of snow but was too thin to hold up the weight of a child, let alone a man. Every year there were accidents. And as if that weren't enough, even as Molly watched, the snowfall was turning to a mixture of snow and freezing rain.

There had been a freezing rain warning on the radio at lunch. Molly never really paid any attention to weather reports except when she was listening to see if school was cancelled. But the adults had been talking about the freezing rain warning because Estelle and Chet had driven up to town and weren't expected back until late in the afternoon. Taid Gareth immediately got into a grumpy mood about young people never being able to sit still for two minutes, and Charlotte had had to put him to bed for his nap as if he were a four-year-old.

Freezing rain. And Molly watched as her cousin — his shirt and long hair flying — disappeared before her eyes in the downpour. She ran for her mother.

Charlotte went out for Keith on the snowmobile. Molly stood with Trick at the window watching Charlotte manhandle the old Ski-Doo over the ice drifts at the river's edge, then gun the motor until she, too, was lost in the veils of wind-driven sleet.

Trick held Molly in his arms. "What's it like having Nanook of the North for a mother?"

He was trying to make Molly feel as though everything were all right. She played along. They watched and waited.

"Why doesn't Taid like the French?" Molly asked.

Her father laughed. "Oh, he's just one of those folks who doesn't like anyone except his own kind. He didn't much like me when your mother first brought me home."

Molly pulled away, astounded, and stared at her father. "Everybody likes you," she said.

Trick laughed again. "Gareth said your mother was making a big mistake marrying an Irishman. Said we were all frivolous drunks and not to be trusted."

"Did you bop him one?" asked Molly.

Trick shook his head. "No. I just told him what my father told me: that the Welsh were only Irishmen who couldn't swim."

Just then Uncle Don came into the study. He had

retired to his bedroom for a nap. "Where is everyone?" he asked.

Trick told him, and Don went through the roof. "My son out in a blizzard! Why didn't someone call me!"

"You know Charlotte," said Trick calmly. "If there's a problem, your sister would rather solve it than think about it."

But Don had thrown down his magazine on a side table and soon could be heard slamming things around in the mud room as he got into his own snowmobile gear.

Molly looked anxiously at her father. "What if he crashes into Mum?"

Trick hugged her again. "Don was born on this river, too," he said.

As it turned out, Don only got as far as the riverbank before Charlotte's headlight beam could be seen heading back to shore through the downpour. Don waited there until he was sure she had Keith with him. Then he gunned his machine back up the hill to the garage and came stomping into the house. Trick met him at the door.

"It looks like everything's going to be okay," said Trick. He and Molly had their arms full of blankets.

Don scowled at his brother-in-law and headed upstairs to his bedroom. Trick called after him, "Don, for Pete's sake, the boy's learned his lesson."

Don stopped on the stairs. "I'm just getting changed," he said. But he didn't come down again.

So it was Uncle Trick who took Keith, numb and trembling, up to his room wrapped in blankets. He sat him on his bed while he ran the boy a bath.

Molly made her mother sit beside the fire in the study. She put on water for tea. Blossom did his part. He flumped down on Charlotte's feet. Then Trick came down, and while the tea was brewing, he poured his wife a brandy. He poured himself one as well. He had a frown on his face.

"Is he okay?" Charlotte asked.

"Who?" said Trick. "Keith's fine. He's up to his ears in hot water. It's his father I'm worried about. He's in his room in a deep freeze."

It was Molly's idea to take Uncle Don a brandy. He was sitting in his bedroom by the window, staring out at the icy shower that beat against the glass. The glass was loose in its frame and wobbled with each new gust. He summoned up a smile for his niece, but his eyes were sad.

Taid Gareth was up when Molly arrived back downstairs. He was shaking his head. "The boy's changed," he said. "Surely you can see that."

"He's sixteen," said Charlotte. "Of course he's changed."

Then they were at it again. Molly slipped quietly away to her room, crawled under the covers, and lost herself in *The Phantom Tollbooth*. Things were pretty crazy in Dictionopolis, but they seemed a lot more pleasant than on Old Bridge Road.

The rain stopped. Molly heard a creaking sound through the wall and realized that Keith was in his room.

She threw back the covers and made her way over to the bookshelf. This had been her mother's room. A lot of her old books were on the shelf. That was where she had found *The Phantom Tollbooth*.

She knelt and looked through the books to see if there was anything a sixteen-year-old might find interesting.

She found something that looked boyish — written by a man, anyway — and before she could change her mind, she slipped out of her room and down the hall to Keith's door. She knocked. There was no reply. She knocked again.

"Enter," he said. His voice was brusque, wary.

He was in bed. He was already reading.

"What is it?" he said.

"I thought maybe you'd like a book," said Molly. "It's called *Heartsease*." She approached the bed.

Keith put down his own book and took the one she offered him.

"I think it's sort of science fiction," said Molly. While he thumbed through it, she glanced at the book on the bedcovers. "*Le dernier des raisins*," she read out loud.

He corrected her pronunciation. "It's for school," he said. Then he showed her something. "Look." In the front of *Heartsease* Nain Maeve had written, "To Donny bach, our darling bookworm, Xmas '70."

Molly examined the inscription. "Donny bach?"

She looked at Keith, who smirked. "Oh, Donny bach, you darling little bookworm," he said. Molly broke up.

She knew that bach meant "little one," if the little one was a boy. She was Molly fach, "little girl." She could remember when Keith had been Keith bach. But he was too big for that now.

Suddenly there was the noise of a car's horn outside, and Molly ran to the window just in time to see Estelle and Chet in his shiny new candy-apple red Honda turn off the Old Bridge Road, spin completely out of control in a lazy 360 — right off the driveway — across the lawn and into Taid Gareth's potting shed.

The temperature had dropped fifteen degrees in less than two hours. Everything was coated with a shiny glaze of ice. The Trans-Canada was a skating rink.

The wreck of the potting shed claimed the lion's share of attention at dinner that evening. Which was unlucky for Chet, but lucky for Keith. His own misadventure on the river earned him only one derisive comment from Taid Gareth, who referred to the episode as Keith's "defection" to the other side, as if Keith were some kind of a traitor running back home to Quebec.

"If you'd drive a *real* car, Chet," said Taid Gareth.

"Oh, come on, Dad!" said Estelle.

"The Honda's a good road handler, Gareth," said Trick.

Gareth huffed. "You think a Jap fancy can handle this climate, do you?"

"Nothing can handle weather like this."

Gareth puffed. "But some good old-fashioned North American *heft* does tend to keep a vehicle on the road."

The grown-ups groaned in unison. Taid Gareth shook his head with showy dismay. "Didn't I teach you clowns anything?"

"You taught us a lot, Dad," said Don. "For one thing, you taught us not to head off across the river on foot alone in a storm."

Charlotte growled at her brother. "And obviously, Dad, you taught us to be *knuckleheaded*," she said, giving Don a withering look.

Keith sulked. Molly threw a pea at him to get his attention. Then she mouthed the words Donny, the darling bookworm, and his sulk thawed out a bit.

Unfortunately the pea did not go unnoticed. "Do not be impudent, young lady," said her mother.

It was that kind of family meal. Everyone pushing everyone else's buttons. Because Estelle and Chet had been late getting back, the roast was dry and the veggies were overdone. And Taid Gareth insisted on having the radio on so he could hear the weather updates. Christmas good cheer was getting stretched pretty thin.

At home Molly knew what to do in this kind of a situation. Ask politely to be excused, remember to carry your plate all the way to the sink — not just to the counter — then slip away to the rec room and watch TV with the volume down low. And tune in something halfway educational — definitely not *Wheel of Fortune*! — so that if Mum or Dad wandered by, they didn't have something new to start lecturing you about.

Unfortunately, Taid Gareth didn't have a TV, which was okay if folks were in a good mood. They could always play cards or Scrabble or, of course, the Tournament.

Molly grabbed Keith just as he was heading upstairs. "You want to play chess?"

He shook his head.

"You have to finish the tournament," she whispered urgently. "There's no way out of it."

He paused on the stairs. "Why isn't there?" he said. But this was a losing battle, and he knew it.

"This is the last round," said Molly. "In two days it's Christmas Eve. It has to be over by Christmas Eve."

Keith took a deep breath. The chess tournament had been Big Argument Number Three. He hated chess. Why should he have to play a game he hated? Because it's what we do, Don told him. It's a Wigstead tradition. Then Keith made the mistake of saying something about being only half a Wigstead, and Don went ballistic.

"I'll let you off easy," said Molly.

Keith grimaced. "If I beat you, nobody'd believe it."

Molly looked horrified. "I didn't mean I'd let you win!" she said. "What I mean is I'll destroy you real quick. So you can get back to your book."

Keith still looked dubious. Molly pleaded. "Don't leave me down here when everybody's being so adultish."

So Keith let her push him back to the study.

Molly set up the players. Behind her back, she hid a white pawn and a black pawn in each hand and then presented her fists to Keith for him to choose. He didn't bother picking. "Just give me black," he said.

Blossom waddled over and plunked himself down on Keith's feet. Blossom didn't play favourites. One set of feet was as good as another.

"I'm no good at this," said Keith as he moved his first pawn.

Molly moved her pawn quickly out to meet him. "I am," said Molly. "But I'll be merciful."

Keith moved another pawn. He looked behind him to see if anyone was hanging around the door. "Taid plays head games on me."

"Like what?" said Molly.

Keith frowned. "He was going on about some duck."

Molly was surprised. "He did that to me, too. And the oboe?"

"Yeah," said Keith. "He was driving me crazy."

Molly moved a piece. "Oh, well," she said, "he's just getting old."

Keith moved a piece. "No way. He was doing it on purpose."

Molly moved her knight out from behind the wall of pawns. She made the knight buck a couple of times, neighed out loud.

Keith stared at her knight. "You're going to laugh, but I never thought of those knights as being, you know, knights."

Molly picked her knight up off the board and held it out for Keith's inspection. "He's on horse-back, Keith," she said, placing the figure back on the board. "What are you using for eyes these days, boy? Currants?" It was one of Taid Gareth's phrases. Keith pulled a face. "Sorry," said Molly.

"I think he pretends he's senile just to throw us off," said Keith.

Molly considered this idea while she contemplated her next move. She didn't want to believe that her grandfather's chatter was deliberately distracting, but she was pretty sure Keith was right. "So maybe I shouldn't neigh and stuff?" she said.

"Do whatever you want."

So, with a good couple of neighs, Molly galloped her knight right over Keith's pawn.

"*Maudit,*" said Keith.

"Try a little bit," said Molly. "Please."

"Okay, okay. It's just that chess was always such a big deal at home. Dad wanting Mum and me to get into the game. We actually had fights about it."

"Yuck," said Molly. "No wonder you're so bad." She picked up her castle. "Taid beat me with just two castles today. But I learned something. They just look like castles. Actually, they're rooks, and that means warrior in some language or other."

Keith had moved another pawn. Now he took Molly's white rook from her and looked it over. "So it's a warrior dressed up like a castle so he can sneak up on you."

"Now you're getting the idea," said Molly. "You've got to think of the players as real people."

She took her knight, made him neigh a couple of more times, then jumped another of Keith's pawns. She made a strangling, death-rattle sound in her throat and made the pawn crawl off the board, where she committed him to Heaven.

"*Tabernacle,*" murmured Keith. Molly stared at him until he looked up self-consciously. "What?"

"Nothing," said Molly, suddenly self-conscious herself.

She looked down at the board, made her move.

"Were you really heading home this afternoon?" she asked without looking up.

Keith looked down at the board. "Don't you start."

"Okay," she said. "I just wondered."

There was a silence while Keith tried to decide where to go next. "That may be Quebec over there, but it's a long, long way from Montreal," he said. He sounded homesick.

"What's it like living there?"

"The same as anywhere."

"It's on the news so much now. We even talked about it in school. About Quebec leaving Canada. Is that going to happen?"

Keith shrugged. He reached down and scruffled Blossom's neck. "Who knows?" he said. "I mean, Montreal's pretty *anglais* anyway. But when Taid says things like 'The only thing wrong with Quebec is the French' — jeez, it's so —"

"Senile?" said Molly.

"No, bigoted," said Keith.

"Is that like stupid?" Molly asked.

Keith smiled. Then his smile faded. Molly was taking one of his bishops. "Hey," he said, "you're just like Taid. Here you are grilling me about stuff, taking my mind off the game and killing me."

Molly smirked and buffed her fingernails on her sweater. It was fun beating adults as long as you were sure they weren't giving you the game. She was pretty sure Keith was playing his best, and that made her feel good. On the other hand, it wasn't much of a challenge.

She watched him bend down close to the board,

try to concentrate. He was really trying. She wondered…The really big challenge would be to let Keith win without him suspecting her. She had never tried to lose before. Could she do it?

It was her move. She made a big point of looking studious. She moved. She began to see a way. She had to make herself open. Let Keith get to her queen. Without her queen, he just might be able to score. But he was on his guard. How could she persuade him he'd won fair and square?

She jumped on another of his pawns. That was it. Play hard around the edges with her knights, bishops and rooks as if she were out for blood. But while she was doing it, clear a path for him to her queen. It would look as if in her greediness, she had inadvertently left herself *wide* open.

She got down on her knees so that her eyes were right at board height. This was going to be exciting.

And she almost did it. She was within a couple of moves of losing when she messed up. Instinctively she moved a player out of a dicey situation and then, realizing what she was doing, moved it back right into a trap. When she looked up, Keith was staring at her, his eyes filled with resentment.

"Thanks so much," he said. "Now I really feel like one of the clan." Then he heaved himself out of his chair.

"Don't go!" said Molly. "I can still beat you if you want."

Keith rolled his eyes and headed for the door, where Taid Gareth appeared, drawn by Molly's cry.

"Leaving us again?" he said.

Keith shook his head in disgust, hurried by his

grandfather, and stomped up the stairs.

Molly pouted.

Taid Gareth came and stared at the board through the smoke blooming out of his pipe. He raised a bushy grey eyebrow. "Such a hothead," he said. "And here he was winning!"

Now it was Molly's turn to leave, not in disgust but in despair and remorse for what she had done.

"What is happening to this family?" said Taid Gareth.

Molly slipped off to the kitchen to cut herself a slice of cake.

She turned off the lights in the kitchen and sat in the dark at the breakfast table in the little nook. The night was as black as the woodstove after Taid had put a fresh coat of polish on it. Steely black but pricked with holes where you could see the light of the fiery stars.

The moon was just a crescent, but it shone down on the hillsides, and there the light seemed to lose its balance on the slippery slopes and slide down onto the river. She looked out at the few blinking lights she could see on the Quebec side. What were those folks doing tonight? Playing chess? Arguing? Watching *Wheel of Fortune* in French?

With the moonlight throwing crumb shadows on her plate, Molly found herself thinking about Nain. Nain Maeve used to make angel food cake as light as moon dust.

When she was dying, the doctors gave her morphine to increase her tolerance to the pain. That struck Molly at the time. Because everyone always talked about how tolerant Nain was just naturally, and Molly had thought that tolerance must be another word for full of life.

What they meant about Nain, Molly had come to learn, was that she put up with Taid Gareth's moodiness and narrow-mindedness.

She really wished Nain were around now.

Molly made her way upstairs. The lights were on in Keith's room. She thought of knocking but changed her mind. She went to her own room. At least she had *The Phantom Tollbooth* to keep her company.

But she didn't turn her light on right away. At home they lived in a suburb, and it was never really dark. She put on her nightgown by the thin, slippery moonlight. It was cool in the old house, but she took her time enjoying a moonbath by the window. There were no other houses around, no one to see her.

Molly was the kind of person who spent a lot of time at windows. And that's why she was the only one in the Wigstead household who saw the second car accident of the day on the Old Bridge Road. A van inched its way down the long, slow-curving hill that passed the house. Suddenly it started wavering around and then, like Chet's car, lost control completely and ploughed deep into the snowbank. Molly watched as the driver tried to free himself, but his front tires spun hopelessly. His back end was in too deep.

The passenger door opened only a fraction, for the snow was up over the bottom of the door. The passenger heaved himself against the door but was unable to open it farther. Then the side door slid open and another man climbed out of the back and jumped down to the ground. The snow was up over his knees. Meanwhile, the front passenger clambered into the back so that he could climb out the sliding door as well. Molly could vaguely make out other figures in the van. The two men dug with their hands and then pushed for all they were worth, but they only managed to get the van stuck more deeply than before.

Molly watched as the driver joined the other two. Three shadowy men talked together, throwing their arms around, slip-sliding on the road. She watched them take notice of the Wigstead house, the only house for miles.

Molly searched for her bathrobe and slippers. Then she ran downstairs.

Already one of the men from the van was at the front door talking to Taid Gareth, or trying to. But nobody understood him. He was speaking French.

Charlotte invited the man to step inside. He was pointing up the road, but from the front door they could not see the van. Taid had thrown up his hands in despair, given up, and slipped to the back of the family crowding around the front door.

"Can't understand a damn word," he said.

That's when Molly stepped in. "Their van's stuck in the snowbank," she said.

The man may not have understood her, but he regarded her as if she had understood him. *"Pouvez-vous nous aider?"* He directed his question only to Molly. But she did not understand what he was saying.

"Il nous faut aller tellement loin," he said. *"On a des nouveaux-nés dans l'auto — trois. Trois bébés. S'il vous plaît, si on pouvait avoir juste un coup de main."*

He sounded so urgent. Molly's mind was racing. She saw her grandfather shake his head. He had an annoyed look on his face.

"Damn frogs. Always after something," he muttered.

Molly felt her face get hot all over. She stamped her foot. "Don't say that!" she said to her grandfather so sharply that he actually jumped.

"Un moment!" she said to the stranger. Then she raced upstairs to Keith's room. She burst through the door without knocking. He was propped up in bed, writing.

Keith looked frightened. "What's wrong?"

Molly tried to catch her breath. "There's a man at the door. He's had an accident. He's French. He can't speak a word of English."

"So?"

"So none of us can speak any French. Only you."

"I can't speak French," he said.

"Yes, you can. You were speaking French when we were playing chess."

"Just swear words."

"And the book," she said. "The one with raisins in the title. Please, Keith. I think there's something really wrong."

Keith looked down. By then Molly had come to his bedside, and — too late — he tried to hide what he had been writing. She grabbed it before he could stop her.

"Hey!" he said.

It was a letter to someone named Annette. *Chère Annette.*

"This is *written* in French!" cried Molly triumphantly. She waved the letter in Keith's face. She took his hand. "Oh, please, Keith," she said. "Try, at least. Taid is being a complete crumb-bum fart."

By the time they reached the door, the man had left. So had Trick, Don and Chet, with flashlights and shovels. Molly was disappointed, but then Charlotte told her that as far as she could make out, there were others in the car — children, maybe — and the men had gone to bring them to the house while they dug out the van.

Molly watched the men helping three women cross the treacherous expanse of shining roadway. Each of the women held an infant tightly in her arms.

"Oh, my God," said Charlotte as she helped them enter the front door. *"Entrez,"* she said, smiling at the women. *"Entrez."*

How tired the women looked. There was a weariness etched deeply into their faces, as if they hadn't slept for days. Estelle and Charlotte led them into the front room. Two of the babies were crying. Taid Gareth took himself off to his study and closed the door after him.

The mothers sat and immediately attended to their children. Newborns they were. Molly got as close as she could. The babies were Chinese-looking. The mothers weren't, but all the babies — one, two, three — were Chinese. And if the clothes were anything to go by, they were all girls.

She looked quizzically at her mother and Estelle, and finally at Keith, who had not yet said a word. He was staring at the three babies.

The women talked very quietly among themselves. Perhaps they'd already been told that there was no one here who could talk to them. Every now and then one of them would look up and smile wearily and say, *"Merci. Merci bien."*

Despite the cold, the front door had been left open. Everyone had been too busy shepherding in the mothers to bother with it. Now Molly was sent to close it. Walking out onto the porch, she could see the men working, making men noises as they each directed who was to do what, where, when and for how long. She heard them all, French and English, and from where she stood, the words were mostly indistinct: the sound of six men digging a van out of a snowbank. She reentered the house shivering and closed the door.

When she joined the women and Keith in the front room, one of the women was changing her tiny Chinese baby on the floor. She was digging out diapers, Vaseline and Baby Wipes from a fat pink change bag. She looked up suddenly and without thinking spoke.

"Est-ce que j'pourrais avoir de l'eau chaude, s'il vous plaît?" she said. Then she said, "Oh," as she realized they could not understand. *"Excusez-moi."*

Molly poked Keith in the side. "Go on," she whispered.

"De l'eau chaude?" said Keith. *"Bien sûr. Avez-vous besoin d'autre chose?"*

All the women in the room stared at Keith with

happy amazement. Molly glowed with pride.

"They need some hot water," Keith said to Estelle.

"Ask them why the babies are Chinese," whispered Molly.

"Shush," he said to her. "Mind your own business."

Then he perched on the edge of a chair and talked to the three mothers. Haltingly sometimes. Sometimes he had to worry the meaning out of a phrase in order to grasp what they were saying. Or they did not quite understand him. Yet they managed. It was obvious there was a lot to say.

At one point Molly noticed that Keith seemed worried. He said *non* a lot and shook his head. He pointed down the road and then back towards the highway, the direction from which they had come. The women grew more and more unhappy.

"What's going on?" Molly asked.

Keith combed his fingers through his long hair. "They think they can cross the river at the Pont d'Entente."

"It's not there anymore!" said Molly.

"That's what I told them," said Keith.

Molly looked at one of the women. Her face appeared to crumble, as if she'd been holding it together for too long and the news about the bridge had been too much. She wept, and the other women comforted her.

Then the men came back. They all were smiling and laughing. They had dug out the van, and Don had even found a couple of concrete blocks to put in the back for extra traction.

"I'm just going to brew up some coffee for

them," said Trick, red-cheeked from a good work-out in the cold. Then they noticed the looks of desolation on the faces of the women.

"*Quoi?*" said one of the men.

Keith explained. "*L'enseigne sur le bâtiment, c'est pas correct. 'Y a plus de pont là-bas. Pas depuis qu'ils ont construit le Trans-Canada.*"

He spoke nervously, glancing up at his father from time to time. Don looked at him with frank amazement.

Charlotte put her arm around her brother's shoulder. "Pretty impressive, eh?"

Hesitantly, Don nodded.

Keith continued then, with more assurance. Bit by bit things were sorted out. Keith translated back and forth.

Trick brought everybody coffee and leftover cake from dinner. Then, when it was determined that the three families could not possibly get back on the road that night, Trick went and got the brandy, and those who wanted had a dram together.

Finally, Taid put in an appearance, looking every bit the master of the house. Blossom was with him. He barked at the excitement, and that made all the babies cry. Molly shushed Blossom up and stroked his fluffy head.

Charlotte took her father aside, led him into the hallway, where the others couldn't hear. But Molly sidled nearby.

"They have to stay," said Charlotte.

"Absolutely not," she heard her grandfather say. "I thought these people wanted their own country. So why should they expect hospitality in mine?"

Molly watched Charlotte with fear and wonder. Her mother did not speak loudly, but she spoke very plainly. "This may be your house, Father. It is also my house, the house I grew up in. There has been a major collision on the Trans-Canada. The police have blocked it off indefinitely. Our guests cannot go north. If they turn around and go south, there isn't a place to stay for miles, assuming they could make it on these roads. I hate to put it this way, but they are leaving this house over my dead body."

Taid Gareth looked daggers at Charlotte, as if maybe her dead body were a possibility. He seemed just about to bluster at her when Molly jumped between them. "I wonder what Nain would have done, Taid," she said. Her grandfather closed his parched old lips tightly. He looked from Molly to her mother and back. There was a betrayed look in his eye.

Then one of the new fathers — Christian, his name was — entered the hall. He seemed to understand what was going on. "*Si ça vous dérange, on peut trouver quelqu'un d'autre. Vous avez déjà fait beaucoup.*"

Keith appeared behind him in the hallway. He looked squarely at his grandfather. "Christian here says if it's, like, a hassle, they'll go. He says you've been really helpful."

Molly watched Taid Gareth's gizzardy throat swallow a couple of times. Then the old man left them there and returned to his study. As he passed her by, Molly could not believe how frail he looked.

Christian, meanwhile, had begun to collect the

others together to leave. Keith stopped them. *"Non! Non! Ça va. Vous êtes bienvenue."*

"Vraiment?"

"Oui, vraiment. Le vieux, y'est juste un peu... b'en, vous savez les vieux..."

Christian smiled, a weary smile. *"Oui, oui."*

Then Molly saw a smirk spread across Keith's face. *"Le problème du Canada, c'est les Canadiens."*

All of the guests laughed, and Christian slapped Keith happily on the back. The travellers agreed to stay the night.

"What did you tell them just now?" said Don to Keith. "What made them laugh so much?"

Keith looked around at his family and took a deep breath. "I told them that the only thing wrong with Canada was the Canadians."

◆

Beds were found for everyone. Cradles were improvised in a chest of drawers, an old radio battery chest, and a dog basket that Blossom had refused ever to sleep in. The grown-ups gave up their rooms to their guests. The Wigsteads decided to camp in the living room.

The guests were exhausted and, with many thanks, retired as soon as they could. The babies would need feeding in the night. Although Molly still had a room to go to, she wasn't going to miss the camp-out for anything. So they all ended up lounging on sleeping bags and lumpy extra pillows and ragged old army blankets. Keith tried to escape to the privacy of his own room but could not go until he had told the story of the Chinese babies.

"Wait," said Don. "I want to hear this, we all

want to hear this! But first, tell us about you."

"What's to know?" said Keith. He looked tired, as if he sensed a trap.

"You haven't been in Montreal all that long," said Don, "and you're bilingual. It's...I don't know...great."

Seeing Keith's face up close, Molly saw the blush even if no one else did.

"Annette!" she said. The secret was out before she could check herself.

Keith gave Molly a pinch for having such a big mouth.

"I have a girlfriend." He shrugged.

"Say no more," said Trick. And everybody laughed.

Then Don said, "Will you introduce me to her if I can get up there sometime?" After only a moment's hesitation, Keith said he would.

He proceeded to tell his family about the Chinese babies. There had been thirty couples from Quebec who had adopted newborn Chinese babies, all girls. Girls were the only thing going. The Quebeckers had flown to China to pick up their children. Christian and his friends had been on the last flight back. They had been flying for more than twenty-four hours.

"Wow!" said Charlotte. "That's a longer delivery than I had with you, Molly."

The couples had to land in Ottawa because of icy conditions in Montreal. Their flight to Rouyn would not be taking off until the following day. Christian and his friends were desperate to get home for Christmas. So they rented the van, thinking they could beat the storm. When the police blocked the Trans-Canada, they drove back to where one of them had noticed the old highway. They saw the sign saying Pont d'Entente and thought they may have found a quick way over to Quebec. They had no idea that the Old Bridge Road went nowhere anymore.

"They would have been stranded," said Trick.

"If it hadn't been for Keith," said Molly. Keith pinched her again. Finally the remaining campers rolled over and tried to get snug. There was a lot of groaning and giggles and shoving. Molly lay in the dark, thinking how amazing it was that adults still knew how to have a sleep-over.

Things eventually quieted down as people drifted off to sleep. And Molly's thoughts drifted to the Chinese babies. She even heard one of them wake up for her bottle. How far they had come to find a home.

There were a few odd stuffed toys in her bedroom. She wondered if her mum would let her give one to each of them. Their first ever Christmas presents.

She slept, and then she woke up. It was still night. She had heard something, a slip, slip, slip sound. It was Taid making his way to the kitchen.

Molly climbed out of her sleeping bag and tiptoed after him. From the kitchen doorway she saw him at the sink getting himself a glass of water. He was taking one of his pills.

"Are you all right, Taid?" she asked.

"Molly fach," he whispered. "What are you doing up?"

She followed him back to the study. There were embers in the fireplace. Taid sat in his La-Z-Boy. Molly sat, too, and they stared sleepily at the dying fire. Taid had a blanket. She didn't think he had gone to bed yet.

"Now you're mad at Keith," she said sadly.

"What makes you say that?"

"Because he can speak French. If he hadn't been able to speak French, the people would have left. You must hate him."

There was a long silence. Molly watched her grandfather's face for a sign. Was he angry at her now? Only the embers of the fire lit up his expression.

"You must think me a very wicked man," he said.

"No," said Molly. "Well, maybe at chess."

There. He smiled.

"I've never hated Keith, child," he said. "But I don't like to see Donald unhappy. He was a moody boy himself. Nain and I worried about him so. Well, I still do. He is still my boy, you see."

"Your Donny bach."

"Yes. My Donny bach."

They sat in silence again. Molly had curled up tight, but she felt cold. She longed for her bed, not the hard floor of the living room. The party was over in there. She found herself thinking how deliciously cool her sheets would be and how she would have to shiver herself warm. She shivered now. Then she slid out of her armchair and gave her grandfather a kiss on his stubbly cheek.

"I think Don is pretty proud of Keith," she said.

"Yes?" said Taid. "Well, that's good then."

•

Molly was the last to wake up. The sun was blasting through her bedroom window. She made her way downstairs to where family and guests were congregated in the huge dining room. A very big breakfast lay in waste there, and Keith was busy translating the many questions everyone seemed to have. The Wigsteads were practising their school French. It was coming back to them with comical results. The guests practised their English. There was some laughter and some teasing, and everyone took a turn holding the babies.

It was still freezing outside, but according to the radio, the Trans-Canada was clear and sanded. It looked as if the Chinese babies would make it home to Rouyn in time for their very first Christmas after all.

Taid was missing from the gathering in the dining room. Molly went looking for him. She was surprised to find him in the study sitting across the game table from Christian.

They were playing chess. Blossom thumped his tail hard on the floor when he saw Molly enter the room. He was sprawled over Christian's feet. Christian hardly seemed to notice. He was intent upon his game.

Taid seemed a bit flustered. It was soon obvious to Molly why. Christian was good.

"You should tell him about the duck, Taid Gareth," said Molly, pulling up a stool. "And why you like oboes so much." She giggled. That did not please her grandfather.

"You know the rules about audience members in the study."

"But this isn't the tournament," said Molly. Taid harrumphed, then leaned back, tapping the arm of his chair in a bothered kind of way.

Despite his inability to distract his opponent, he was playing a good game. He had a confident look on his face. Molly checked the board. Taid Gareth's bishop was poised for a lethal attack. Two moves, and he would have Christian cornered.

Last night it had been too difficult for Molly to remember any of what little French she had learned yet in school. But now she could remember some. She had a plan. She would touch Gareth's bishop on the head and ask Christian what the French word was for it. Once he looked at the piece, maybe he would see the danger he was in. She rehearsed the words in her mind. *"Comment appelez-vous cela?"* Her hand stretched out across the board, but before she was even near the bishop, Christian gently brushed her hand out of the way.

"Non, non!" he said.

Obediently Molly put her hands in her lap. She glanced at Taid, whose furry eyebrows were low over his eyes.

"Whatever were you thinking, Molly fach?" he said. But there was a glimmer in his eyes that was far from senile.

"Le — how you say? — game," said Christian, "must be fair, *non?*"

He looked from Molly to her grandfather. They both nodded.

Christian folded his hands in front of his face as

if in prayer, and he looked hard at the board. Then he looked at Molly again with a playful glint in his eye and wagged his finger, mock scolding her.

Molly looked at her grandfather. He was smiling. "She's a little vixen, Monsieur Christian," he said.

"Ah!" said Christian, though it did not seem that he had understood what a vixen might be. For that matter, Molly didn't know herself.

He returned his gaze to the board and made a good move. The bishop — for the moment — was stalled.

Taid Gareth cursed under his breath in Welsh, but there was no force behind it. He pretended to bop Molly on the top of her head with his pipe.

Christian laughed, pointing at her but directing his question at her grandfather. *"Vous devez être bien fier d'elle?"*

"Oh, God," muttered Taid. "What's he going on about now?"

Christian searched his mind. "Uh, pride? *Elle est bien, non?"*

"Ah," said Taid Gareth, comprehension flowering on his face. "Am I proud of you, Molly?"

She nodded and moved beside him, where he could slip his arm around her.

"You were going to give me away, weren't you, you little traitor?" he mumbled in a gruff voice that didn't scare her one bit.

She very carefully buttoned up his lip.

The game was declared a draw. It was too close, the competitors too equally matched. Besides, the new parents were anxious to get back on the road.

There were many hugs and handshakes and

promises at the door. Gareth stood well back from the commotion, but Christian came to him and shook his hand solemnly. He spoke to him at length, urging Keith to translate for him.

"He said, if your car should break down on some cold winter night in Rouyn, you will always be welcome in his home, where he will gladly beat the pants off you in chess."

Gareth had to laugh.

"What do you think?" said Molly.

Gareth thought a moment. Then he said, *"Dyna beth sydd iti wybod: bydd yn agored."*

No one knew what he meant. Don, who was the oldest, said, "It's Welsh, but I couldn't make it out."

"Molly will tell you," said Taid Gareth.

Molly looked wide-eyed at him.

"It's what I warned you about the other day, when we were playing," said her grandfather.

She whispered it in Keith's ear, and Keith translated it into French for the departing guests. They smiled and clapped. One of the mothers kissed Gareth on both cheeks, French style.

"What does it mean?" Don asked his son when the guests had driven off and the Wigsteads were alone again.

But Keith was tired of translating, so he left it up to Molly to explain.

"Here's what we need to know," she said. "Be open."